CITY FARM

Katie and the Ducklings

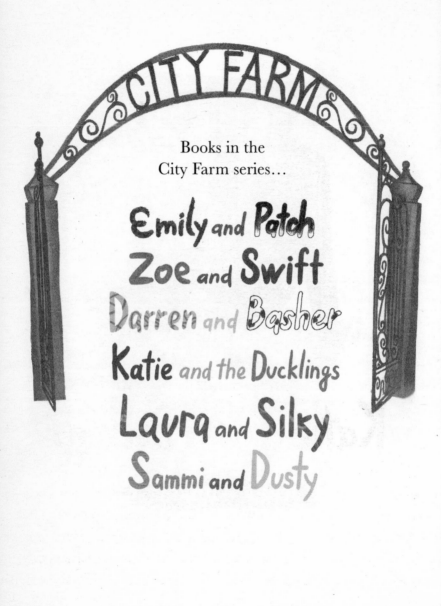

CITY FARM

# Katie and the Ducklings

Jessie Williams

Special thanks to
Kate Cary

First published in 2013 by Curious Fox,
an imprint of Capstone Global Library Limited,
7 Pilgrim Street, London, EC4V 6LB
Registered company number: 6695582

www.curious-fox.com

Text © Hothouse Fiction Ltd 2013

Series created by Hothouse Fiction
www.hothousefiction.com

The author's moral rights are hereby asserted.

Illustrations by Dewi@kja-artists

ISBN 978 1 78202 023 3

1 3 5 7 9 10 8 6 4 2

A CIP catalogue for this book is available from the British Library.

Typeset in Baskerville by Hothouse Fiction

Printed and bound in the United Kingdom by CPI

For Dylan.

# Prologue

Katie dragged her school sweatshirt from the dirty washing basket and tried to ignore its stale smell. Mum hadn't got round to doing any washing all weekend but Katie didn't want to complain because she didn't want to upset her. It was hard enough getting Mum out of bed to drive her to school these days; if she complained about her smelly sweatshirt, Mum might just hide under the covers again.

Katie picked the crusty ketchup off the sleeve and brushed out the chalk marks, then she peeked out of her bedroom, wishing she could smell breakfast cooking. But there was only the smell of last night's fish fingers. The hall light wasn't even on. Mum must still be in bed. Padding softly to the bathroom, Katie reached for her toothbrush, squeezed out some toothpaste and began cleaning her teeth. A few months ago, Mum would have been downstairs by now, singing along to the radio while she whipped up a batch of muffins or a stack of pancakes. Mum loved cooking, and she always used to pile the breakfast table with delicious treats to make Katie smile before school.

That's how it used to be. Now Katie felt like her old mum was disappearing. It was scary. Katie had no dad to fill in the gaps. If Mum disappeared, she'd be all alone.

She pushed the thought away and spat out the toothpaste.

If only Mum hadn't lost her job.

That's when everything had started to change. Mum hadn't stopped baking straightaway. Katie stared wistfully into the bathroom mirror as she remembered Mum's double-chocolate-chip-marble-cheesecake and her super-special-cupcakes whirled with icing and sparkling with sprinkles. When she'd first lost her job, Mum had seemed more filled with energy than ever, applying for jobs and travelling to interviews. There was always a pile of job application forms stacked neatly on the dining-room table, usually next to a plate full of freshly baked buns. But gradually Mum had stopped looking for work. Then she'd stopped baking. Now she hardly left the house. She hardly left her bed.

*Please let Mum get up today and take me to school.* Katie brushed her teeth harder. *If I scrub off every bit of plaque*, Katie begged the Tooth Fairy, *please make her get up and drive me to school.* Of course Katie knew the Tooth Fairy didn't exist. She was nearly eleven. But there was no one else to ask. She rinsed her mouth out with water. She couldn't miss this week's spelling test. She'd missed last week's test; Mum hadn't felt well enough to get up and drive her to school. This week Katie had learned every word on her spelling list. She was determined to prove that she could keep up, even though she'd missed so many lessons recently.

If only school was closer, she could walk there. Katie put her toothbrush back into the pot beside the tap. Perhaps she could learn to take the bus. But Mum had stopped giving her pocket money weeks ago so she didn't have any money for her bus fare.

She came out of the bathroom and looked at her watch. Eight o'clock. Mum's room was still dark. Then Katie had an idea. Creeping downstairs, she flicked on the kitchen light. The weather outside looked chilly and dull. Katie tucked her feet into her fluffy slippers and put the kettle on. If she woke Mum with a nice cup of coffee, it might cheer her up; and then she'd get up and drive Katie to school in time for registration.

Nervously, Katie waited while the kettle rumbled to a boil. She reached into the cupboard for the coffee jar and spooned some into a mug. Tipping the kettle carefully, she filled the mug, added a splash of milk from the fridge and carried the coffee carefully upstairs.

'Mum?' She paused outside Mum's bedroom door, and then pushed it open. Inside was dark and it smelled fusty, like Katie's sweatshirt.

On the ruffled bed, a mound of duvet moved a little.

'Mum?' Katie tiptoed closer. 'I've brought you a cup of coffee.'

Mum peered over the duvet and rubbed her eyes. 'What?'

'I hope it's going to be sunny later,' Katie said brightly, ignoring the dark rings under Mum's eyes. 'Because it's games this afternoon and we're playing football on the outdoor pitch.' She carefully stepped over a pile of clothes heaped beside the bed. Clearing a space on the cluttered bedside table, she put down the coffee. The mug was starting to burn her fingers.

'Hello, love.' Katie recognized Mum's pretend-happy voice. Mum heaved herself up into a sitting position and piled some pillows behind her head before sinking back against them.

'Shall I open a window?' Katie asked. Maybe some fresh air might make her mum want to go outside.

'What time is it?' Mum yawned.

Hope flickered in Katie's chest as she made a crack between the curtains and opened the window just wide enough to let in a little air. 'Quarter past eight. If you get up now we can still get to school on time.'

Mum sighed. 'School.' She looked wearily at Katie. 'I'm not really feeling too good, Katie. Why don't you stay home today? You can always do some reading here.'

'I have to go.' Katie stared at her mum. 'I have a spelling test.'

Mum frowned. 'But I'm not feeling well enough to drive.'

'You look OK.' Katie picked up the mug of coffee. If she could just get her mum to take a sip she might feel a bit better. Katie knew her mum wasn't actually ill. Her sadness had just got so big it felt too heavy to move. 'Here.' She held out the coffee.

But Mum didn't see it. She was too busy rubbing

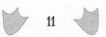

her eyes. Katie gasped as Mum's elbow collided with the mug, sending coffee splashing across the duvet.

Katie froze. She watched the brown liquid spread over the cream cotton and sink in. 'I'm sorry!' she cried.

Mum's face crumpled. 'Oh no! Look at the mess. What am I going to do?'

Katie felt her throat tighten. Why couldn't Mum go back to being the nice mum who made pancakes and buns and who always knew what to do? 'I'm really sorry.' She felt her lip start to tremble. 'I was just trying to—'

'Please! Leave me alone. I told you, I'm not feeling well. I just need to be left in peace.' Mum wriggled back under the coffee-stained duvet.

'But what about school?'

'It won't hurt you to miss it for once,' Mum mumbled from beneath the duvet.

'But it's not just once! It's nearly every day!' Angrily, Katie fumbled for the door behind her. Tears spilled down her cheeks as she raced for her bedroom, choking back sobs.

# Chapter One

'Where's my favourite picture?' Asha searched the wall of bright paintings for the pretty crayon sketch of Bubble and Squeak – City Farm's guinea pigs. She spotted its familiar colours showing beneath a fresh painting of a fat, orange pig. 'Can I move this?' She turned to Rory, who was stamping mud from his boots on the doormat as he held the door of the barn open.

'Move what?' Rory stepped inside, letting the door swing shut behind him. He pulled off his woolly hat.

Asha grinned as his curly white hair sprang out, like piles of cotton wool on his head. 'This new painting of Cynthia.' She pointed to the pig picture. 'It's hiding Bubble and Squeak.'

'As long as you find somewhere else to put it,' Rory replied.

 13

Jack scrambled off the sofa beside the stove and pointed to a spot above Kerry's desk. 'It can go *there*.'

Rory scratched his head. 'Perhaps you should ask Kerry first.' Rory Trent was the farm manager. He was more used to being outside, cleaning the pens and seeing to the animals. Inside the cosy barn, he let Kerry take charge.

Jack pointed to the grey wall chart over Kerry's desk. 'If we put pictures around that, it'll brighten up the whole wall.'

Jack had been at City Farm even longer than Asha. She knew that he'd joined the farm's Harvest Hope project after being bullied at his new school, though it was hard to believe that anyone could bully the grinning ten-year-old who grabbed the pig painting from Asha and raced over to Kerry's desk.

Balancing on her chair he pinned the picture above the wall chart. 'That looks better,' he said, jumping down and admiring his work.

Asha nodded approvingly at the pig picture on Kerry's wall. It really did brighten up the office corner of the old barn. The barn was Asha's favourite part of the whole farm. Rory had told her that once, a long time ago, it had looked out onto rolling fields as far as the eye could see. But the city had crept up around it and hemmed the whole farm in with roads and buildings. Asha loved the way the barn stood firm, guarding the paddocks and stables as though it was telling the city that the farm was never moving, no matter what. Asha gazed up past the rafters to the barn's wonky roof. It matched the uneven walls, where ancient diamond-paned windows let in yellowing light. In the centre of the barn, where Asha was sitting, three battered sofas huddled around a warm stove. Kerry's desk, cluttered with paper, sat behind them and, through an opening beside the craft tables at the far side of the barn, Asha could see the farm café.

She sniffed hopefully. 'I wonder how Kerry's cakes are going.'

As she spoke, Kerry rushed out of the café. She was holding a hot tray with a tea towel. 'Ow! Ow! Ow!' With a gasp she dropped it onto a craft table. 'Cupcakes anyone?' she asked, blowing on her fingers.

'Are you OK?' Asha asked anxiously.

'I'm fine.' The beads in Kerry's plaited hair clacked around her shoulders. 'But unfortunately I can't say the same for the cakes.'

Asha looked at the tray. They didn't look like the cupcakes Daisy baked when she ran the farm café. Daisy's cakes rose up from their baking trays like mini-mountains, cracked at the summit to show the soft sponge inside. But Daisy had retired last week and Clive, the man who was supposed to have been taking over from her, had cancelled at the last minute. Asha still remembered the horrified look on Kerry's face when Rory patted her on the shoulder and said, 'I'm afraid it's your job until we can find someone else.'

Looking at Kerry's cupcakes now, Asha understood why she didn't want to take over the cooking. Kerry was brilliant at running the Harvest Hope project for children who were finding life difficult. Kerry could take any kid, and no matter how unhappy, anxious, or angry they were, she'd make them feel welcome, special, and happy again. Asha remembered how fed-up she'd felt when she first arrived at City Farm. She was one of Harvest Hope's first recruits after she'd been very ill with leukaemia. Working with Kerry and Rory and the animals had made her feel so much better after being stuck in a hospital bed for months. Yes, Kerry was definitely a lot better at helping kids than at baking. Her cupcakes were wonkier than the barn roof, and burned on one side, pale on the other. A couple had sunk completely. Some had tried to rise but their middles had collapsed as though they'd simply died in the oven.

'Perhaps if we ice them, they'll look a bit better,' Asha suggested.

'I iced the batch I made before.' Kerry disappeared into the café and returned with a plate of uneven cakes, dripping with coloured icing that oozed onto the plate into rainbow puddles. She offered one to Jack.

'Er, thanks.' He took one nervously.

Kerry held out the plate to Asha.

'Thank you.' Asha picked the smallest one. 'I'm sure they taste lovely.' She took a bite and tried to smile. The cake was dry and tasted like sawdust.

*Beep! Beep! Beep!*

'Smoke alarm!' Rory leaped to his feet.

Kerry's face froze. 'My cookies!' She raced back into the café, where a cloud of smoke was filling the air.

As soon as she disappeared, Asha took a pack of tissues from her bag, wrapped one round Kerry's cake and slid it into her pocket. 'I'm sure she'll get better at the baking with some practice.'

'I hope so.' Jack stared sadly at his cake.

Asha handed him a tissue.

'Perhaps Cynthia will like it. She eats pretty much anything.' Jack folded his cake in the tissue and hid it in his pocket.

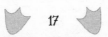

17

Rory clapped Jack on the back. 'Cynthia will love it – she'll think it's her birthday.'

He quickly hushed as Kerry trudged out of the kitchen. A tray hung limply from her oven-mitted hand. There were eight black discs welded onto it.

'The cookies?' Asha asked gently.

Kerry sighed. 'They were supposed to be.'

Rory pulled on his woolly hat. 'Never mind. Arthur can use them on the vegetable patch. He swears charcoal keeps the slugs at bay.'

'Charcoal,' Kerry repeated sadly. 'They were meant to be chocolate chip.' She slid the tray onto her desk and glanced at her wall calendar. She didn't notice the pig picture hanging proudly above it. Instead she ran her finger down the week, stopping as she reached today. 'Oh, gosh, Katie's meant to be here!'

Asha grinned. She'd forgotten a new girl was starting at the Harvest Hope project today. She really liked meeting new recruits. They always had interesting stories to tell, even if it took a while before they were ready to tell them. And she couldn't wait to show Katie Bubble and Squeak. And the lambs. And Fifi's brood of fluffy yellow chicks. This was the best time of year to start helping at City Farm. There'd soon be an early crop of peas to pinch from

 18

the vegetable patch. Arthur the gardener complained if he caught them picking pods, but Asha could tell by the twinkle in his eye that he was secretly pleased to see the children snacking on his healthy crops instead of stuffing themselves with sweets and crisps.

Jack raced to a window and peered out across the yard. 'What time is she meant to be here?'

'Nine o'clock.' Kerry looked at her watch. 'It's quarter past now.'

Rory headed for the door. 'I'll go and check the yards. Make sure the lass hasn't got lost.'

As Rory disappeared out of the barn, Asha turned to Kerry. 'Why's Katie joining Harvest Hope?'

Jack climbed onto one of the battered sofas and leaned over the back to listen.

'She's been off sick from school a lot,' Kerry explained.

Asha felt a prickle of worry. 'Is it anything serious?' She remembered how scared she'd been when she'd first got her leukaemia diagnosis. Especially when she'd seen how frightened her parents were.

'Is she being bullied?' Jack stuck out his chest as though he was ready to take on anyone who dared bully Katie. 'Is that why she's not going to school?'

'No,' Kerry reassured them. 'But her teacher

thought it would do her good to work in the fresh air for spring half term.' She looked at her watch again. 'I just hope she won't start missing days here as well as at school.'

Asha recognized the anxious look in Kerry's eyes. If Katie didn't come to City Farm how could they help her feel better? 'Don't worry.' She rushed over and grabbed Kerry's hand. 'She's probably just missed her bus, or her mum and dad's car won't start. I'm sure she'll be here soon.'

Kerry smiled at Asha. 'You're probably right. Why don't we go out to the gates and look out for her?' She looked at her watch again. 'If she's not here in fifteen minutes, I'll phone her mum and check everything's OK.'

# Chapter Two

Katie looked at her watch.

*Nine-fifteen.*

She was late.

Mum had slept through the alarm. She was still asleep now and they should have left half an hour ago.

Katie drummed her fingers nervously on the kitchen table.

*Mum will be upset if I wake her now.* Her stomach knotted. *She'll say it's too late to go. Then she'll start crying and worrying that she's let me down again.*

Katie put her empty cereal bowl in the dishwasher.

*Why didn't I wake her earlier?*

She rinsed her juice glass under the tap.

*She'd have found an excuse not to drive me to City Farm.*

 21

Katie put the cereal packet back in the cupboard. Her hands felt clammy. The people at City Farm would be waiting for her. Would they be cross that she hadn't arrived?

*I'll walk there.*

The thought hit Katie like a sudden burst of sunshine. It was the perfect solution! She wouldn't have to wake Mum.

Katie tugged open a drawer and fished out a pen. She ripped yesterday's page from the cat calendar beside the microwave and scribbled on the back:

*Gone to City Farm.*
*Lots of love.*
*Katie xxx*

She crept upstairs into Mum's room and left the note on her bedside table. Mum was curled under the duvet, her back to the door.

'Bye, Mum,' Katie whispered and she headed downstairs.

Outside, it had been raining. The pavements were wet, but the clouds were beginning to clear. Katie had seen City Farm from the car. Mum used to drive past it on the way to the cinema. It wasn't far. She hunched into her anorak and set off up the road. Remembering Mum's route, she turned left onto the high street.

She walked past shops, scanning for road signs that might help her find her way. The only signs she could see told motorists where they could park. She knew that she had to turn up a side street. Mum called it her special short cut, but Katie couldn't remember which street it was. Then she spotted a narrow road cutting between the chemist and the newsagent. It was lined with cars. Katie headed up it, hoping she'd made the right turn. But the street wound on, and the houses around her looked less and less familiar. The pavement began to slope up, steepening into a sharp hill. This definitely wasn't the way.

Katie looked at her watch again.

*Nine-twenty-five.*

She wasn't even *close* to the farm. She raced back to the high street. Bursting out beside the chemist, she looked around in panic. With a rush of relief she spotted a sign near the traffic lights further down: *City Farm*! It was pointing down a narrow road. Katie raced for the pelican crossing and hit the button, shuffling her feet impatiently as she waited for the red man to turn green. When it did, she scooted across the road, butterflies whirling in her stomach, and followed the sign to City Farm.

This narrow road looked familiar. It was lined with factories and office blocks. Grass sprouted up between the kerbstones. Breaking into a run, Katie raced past blank buildings and chain-link fences. She recognized a left turn and took it, passing a row of terraced houses before the road crossed a railway line and wound once more between sprawling factories. Her heart pounded in her chest. The wind tugged at her hood.

*Was this really the right way?*

Her footsteps echoed as she sprinted past a dull-grey warehouse. She rounded the corner and her eyes widened. A wire fence enclosed a wide yard. Behind it, she could see patches of green. Wooden planters sprouting daffodils clustered around a gate. Above it, sunshine flashed off brightly painted sign:

*CITY FARM*

Katie looked at her watch again.

*Nine-thirty.*

Next time she wouldn't be late. She'd leave early. It didn't matter if Mum stayed asleep. She could get here by herself. But she was so late. Would the City Farm staff be cross? If only Mum was here to explain.

Swallowing the lump rising in her throat, she lifted her chin and pushed her way through the gate.

The yard opened ahead of her. Gardens, still bedraggled from winter, crowded the edge. But where should she go? Katie tried to remember the letter City Farm had sent to Mum. It explained everything about her first day on the Harvest Hope project, including where to sign in. But she'd left it at home, sitting among the other papers piled on the kitchen counter.

Katie's palms tingled. She began to cross the yard.

'Katie?'

A voice made her jump.

'Are you Katie?' A man in wellies and a woolly hat appeared at the side of the yard, emerging from a gap between two rows of tangled bushes. He waved and smiled, his rosy cheeks glistening like apples in the damp wind.

Katie nodded, not sure what to say, and hurried to meet him.

'Everything OK, lass? We thought we'd lost you.'

Katie hunched deeper into her anorak. 'Sorry I'm late,' she mumbled.

'No problem. No problem at all.' He gave her a twinkly-eyed smile. 'I'm Rory, the farm manager. Pleased to meet you.' He glanced past her into the yard, as if he was looking for something. 'Did your mam bring you?'

Katie flushed. 'She dropped me off,' she said quickly. 'At the gate. She was in a rush. She was on her way to a job interview.' She hated lying but she didn't want anyone to know Mum was still at home, in bed, asleep.

'Never mind,' Rory said breezily. 'We can meet her next time.'

Katie avoided his gaze. 'Yes.'

'I should take you straight to Kerry,' Rory murmured. His thoughts seemed to be somewhere else. 'She runs the Harvest Hope project.'

Katie shoved her hands in her pockets, feeling even more nervous.

'But…' Rory rubbed his nose, 'I suppose there's no harm in her waiting a few more minutes. There's something I want to show you.' He ducked back through the tangled bushes and beckoned at Katie to follow him. On the other side of the bushes was a muddy path. They walked along it until they reached a wooden gate beside a honeysuckle bush. It hung wonkily on rusty hinges and squeaked when Rory pushed it open.

'Just before you arrived, I spotted two pied wagtails flying towards the orchard here.' Rory lowered his voice as he led Katie through the gate. 'I reckon they were heading for the bird table. Shall we see if we can spot them?'

Katie stared at the orchard. The trees were all dressed in snowy spring blossom. A gust of wind sent flurries of petals drifting down onto the grass like confetti.

'It's beautiful!' Katie gasped.

'Aye. We'll have plenty of apples and pears come the autumn,' Rory said with a smile.

At the far end of the orchard, Katie spotted a wooden bird table, where a crowd of small brown birds were squabbling over seeds. She knew that pied wagtails were black and white. She searched the twittering brown mob for a flash of white. 'I can't see them,' she whispered to Rory.

Rory frowned. 'I'm sure they were heading this way, I—'

'There!' Katie cut him off as a tiny flicker of black showed among the blossom of one of the trees. Two wagtails were flitting between the branches. They made the petals shiver as they hopped along the branch.

'Well spotted, lass.' Rory crouched beside her. 'They're watching the table.'

The wagtails eyed the crowded bird table, then, one at a time, fluttered from the branch and pushed

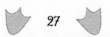

their way in among the other birds.

'Katie?' A loud voice sounded from the gate. 'Is that you?'

The birds scattered as a tall, black woman came into the orchard. Her hair was woven into dozens of plaits, brightly beaded at the ends. Her long skirt fluttered around her ankles.

Katie nodded and stiffened. She wished she could fly away too.

'Hello, Katie. I'm Kerry.' The woman smiled and walked towards her. 'I'm glad you're here.' She looked at Rory. 'I was about to phone her mum. I thought—'

'There's no need to phone her,' Katie butted in.

'Her mam's at a job interview.' Rory rested his hand on Katie's shoulder. 'She just dropped Katie off. We've been doing a spot of bird-watching.'

'Have you found her?' Footsteps pattered along the path and a girl with a thin face and wide smile burst through the gate. A bright flowery hat covered her hair. 'Yay! You're here! Hello, I'm Asha.' She tugged a sandy-haired boy in after her. 'And this is Jack.'

'Hi, Katie.' Jack smiled over the top of a bright blue scarf that was wrapped snugly under his chin.

'Hello,' Katie answered shyly.

'Bird-watching?' Kerry gazed around the

garden, her eyes bright. 'Have you spotted anything interesting?'

'Pied wagtails,' Rory told her. 'Katie spotted them.'

'Wagtails?' Asha squeaked. 'I love wagtails! Where are they?'

Rory chuckled. 'A herd of elephants scared them off.'

'Elephants?' Jack looked puzzled.

'I think he means us,' Kerry said. 'Sorry, Rory.' Then she beckoned to Katie. 'Let me show you the barn. That's where I usually start the tour.' She waved Asha and Jack towards Rory. 'Why don't you start work and we'll catch you up when I've shown Katie around?'

Asha waved goodbye. 'OK, Kerry.'

Katie followed Kerry out of the orchard, unzipping her anorak. She was still warm from running to the farm and the cool breeze felt good as it billowed through her jacket.

They ducked past the bushes and began to cross the yard. Chickens were streaming across it, pecking at the ground. The yard was paved with old stones, thick with mud. The mud splashed Katie's trainers but she hardly noticed. She was watching the chickens warily. They squawked and fluttered as Kerry waded through them. Katie followed, keeping close.

'Here we are,' Kerry announced. 'The barn.'

Katie looked up. Kerry was holding open the door of a huge tumbledown building. Its great roof arched against the sky and reached low, sheltering the weather-beaten, stone walls where diamond-paned windows glittered in the sunshine. The barn looked ancient, like a weary old bear.

Katie followed Kerry inside. She was surprised by how cosy the barn was. There were sofas and a stove and the walls were crowded with colourful paintings, which fluttered as they passed.

'Wait a moment.' Kerry crossed the barn and searched through a stack of papers on a desk at the far end.

Katie waited beside the sofas. She could smell something strange. 'Is something burning?' she asked.

Kerry looked up with a sheepish grin. 'Ah, that was my fault. I was trying to do some baking for the café but I'm afraid I'm not exactly the world's greatest cook.' She pulled a pink pamphlet out of the pile and waved it at Katie. 'Did you get one of these with the letter I sent you?'

Katie shook her head. 'I don't think so.' She wondered if Mum had put it somewhere when she opened the letter and forgotten about it.

'It's just some stuff about the Harvest Hope project,' Kerry explained. She held it out to Katie. 'Take it home and give it to your mum. It's got our phone number on the back so she can call us if you're going to be late again.'

Katie felt herself flush as she took the pamphlet. 'Thanks.'

Kerry sat on the back of one of the sofas. 'So, what do you know about the project?'

'Is it for kids who miss a lot of school?' Katie guessed.

'It's for kids with all sorts of problems.' Kerry looked thoughtful. 'Kids that are sad and angry or finding life difficult to cope with.' Her brown eyes softened. 'Kids like you.'

Katie shifted her feet. She wasn't finding life difficult. Mum was. She lowered her eyes so Kerry couldn't tell what she was thinking. No one could know that Mum was the reason she'd been missing school. If they did, Mum would get in trouble. Her cheeks started to burn. But just at that moment, the barn door crashed open and Jack raced in.

'Something really terrible's happened!' he shouted.

Rory strode in behind Jack, shaking his head. 'It's bad news, I'm afraid.'

# Chapter Three

Kerry jumped to her feet. 'What is it?'

'A fox got into the duck house last night,' Jack exclaimed.

Rory's shoulders slumped. 'Speckles and Quackers are gone.'

'Gone?' Katie stared at him. 'But how do you know a fox got them? Maybe they just escaped?'

Jack shook his head. 'There's a hole, burrowed under the shed.'

'It must have been a fox,' Rory said glumly.

Katie gasped. 'Will it kill them?'

Jack stared at her, his eyes widening with surprise. 'Of course!'

Kerry touched Katie's shoulder. 'I'm so sorry this has happened on your first day, Katie.'

'I guess I'm just used to it.' Jack loosened his scarf. 'It happened a lot on my grandad's farm.'

Katie blinked. 'You live on a farm?'

'I used to,' Jack explained. 'Grandad had to sell Hilltop when he got too old to do the heavy work.'

Rory ruffled Jack's hair. 'Which was lucky for us. Jack here knows more about farming than anyone.'

Jack scuffed his foot on the carpet. 'Well, I know foxes can't resist chicken coops or duck pens.'

'We have to make it more secure,' Rory said.

'We could dig a trench round the edge of the shed,' Jack suggested. 'And bury chicken wire deeper than foxes can burrow.'

'Good idea.' Rory reached under his woolly hat and scratched his head. 'Even foxes can't dig through wire.'

Katie couldn't stop thinking about the lost ducks. 'Poor Quackers and Speckles. Why would a fox do something like that?'

'It probably had cubs to feed,' Jack said.

Rory turned back to the door. 'Come on, Jack, lad. Let's get to work.'

Jack hurried after him. 'I'll fetch a roll of chicken wire from the store.'

Rory opened the door. 'Can you manage it by yourself?'

'I'll get Asha to help me.'

As the door swung shut after them, the phone on Kerry's desk started to ring.

'Hello, City Farm,' Kerry said into the receiver in a sing-song voice. 'Oh, hello, Mr Jarvis.'

Katie looked over at her, wondering why her voice had suddenly gone so serious.

'No, not yet,' Kerry said with a frown, 'but we will be able to keep the café open until we find a replacement. I've been doing the baking myself.' Kerry raised her eyebrows as she listened to the person on the other end of the phone. 'I can assure you, Mr Jarvis, that I'm a very good cook.' She winked at Katie and crossed her fingers, but then she started to frown. 'OK, fine, you do that!' She slammed the phone down. 'Honestly, that man!' she exclaimed.

'Who was it?' Katie asked shyly.

'Derrick Jarvis.' Kerry came out from behind her desk and walked over to Katie. 'He's the finance manager for the council. It's his job to make sure we don't cost the council too much money – and to make my life hell,' she added with a laugh. 'He's worried because our café manager left last week and we still don't have a replacement for her. We make most of our money from the café.' Kerry buttoned up her coat. 'But you don't need to hear about all of that, let me show you the farm before the whole day has gone.' She glanced at Katie's mud-spattered trainers. 'You're going to need some wellies.' She led Katie over to a low shelf beside the door. It was scattered with scarves and gloves, and beneath it was a row of wellington boots. 'What size are you?' Kerry reached for a pair.

'Three.' Katie began to slip off her trainers. The floor felt chilly through her socks.

Kerry looked at the bottom of the wellies she was holding. 'Seven! You'll drown in these.' She scanned the welly line and pulled out another pair. 'Jackpot!' she called cheerfully as she looked at the soles. 'Size three.' She handed the pair of red wellies to Katie.

Katie slipped them on. They felt even chillier than the floor. 'They're cold!'

'You'll soon have them warm,' Kerry promised her, pushing the door open.

As Katie headed after her into the yard, a fresh wind whipped her cheeks. Above, the clouds had cleared and she pushed her hair back. It was good to feel the sun on her face. Katie hurried after Kerry along a gravel path, the stones crunching beneath her wellies, away from the yard and past a higgledy-piggledy garden.

An old lady was crouched over a flower bed, snipping at a bush with a rusty pair of clippers. She trimmed a shoot and pushed it into a small pot of earth. Behind her, there was a whole tray of pots, each holding a fresh cutting.

Kerry waved at the lady. 'Hello, Mrs James!'

Mrs James waved back. 'I've got some wonderful cuttings for the farm shop!' she called happily.

'Great!' Kerry answered. She glanced back at Katie. 'That's the flower garden. We sell the cuttings on our plant stall to raise money for the farm. Derrick Jarvis will be pleased.'

The path veered past a wide vegetable plot. Long rows of freshly dug soil were dotted with young plants. A tattered scarecrow leaned at the centre, its ragged clothes flapping in the breeze. Beanpoles lined one bed. Kerry pointed to the green tendrils that were beginning to climb up them. Look, the broad beans have sprouted.'

Katie had to squint to see them; blinding sunshine was bouncing off a greenhouse at the edge of the plot.

'We grow everything you can think of here,' Kerry told her. 'Potatoes, onions, cabbages, carrots.'

A loud grunt interrupted her.

'Hello, Cynthia.' Kerry stopped beside a low wall.

The small yard beyond was scattered with straw and a huge orange pig was lumbering towards them from the shed at the end.

Squealing loudly, Cynthia heaved her forelegs onto the top of the wall. Katie took a step back. The pig didn't look very friendly.

Kerry leaned forward and scratched the ginger hair sprouting between the pig's ears. 'How's my favourite pig?' She pulled an apple core from her pocket and chucked it onto the straw. 'There you go.'

Cynthia gulped it down.

Katie stared at her nervously. 'I didn't know pigs were so big.'

'They're not all as big as Cynthia,' Kerry said. 'You can give her a pat if you like. I know she looks pretty grumpy but she's a big softy really. Jack loves her.'

*Pat a pig?* Katie shrank back even further. 'Doesn't she bite?'

Kerry laughed. 'No. She's used to visitors and Jack's always playing with her. He's even taught her how to kick a football!'

Katie giggled at the thought of a footballing pig. Then, cautiously, she reached over the wall and touched Cynthia's head. She was surprised how warm and soft it felt. Cynthia snuffled and lifted her head. Katie pulled her hand away quickly as Cynthia hooked her forelegs over the wall and started sniffing her jacket.

'I think she likes you.' Kerry grinned.

'Really?' Katie kept one eye on Cynthia's glistening snout. 'I'm not used to farm animals.'

'You soon will be.' Kerry started heading off. 'Come and meet our racehorse.'

'Racehorse?' Katie chased after her until a loud bleat made her stop. 'Oh, look!' In a pen beside the path, a fat sheep was lying in straw, eyes closed, while a lamb clambered onto her back and balanced there on long woolly legs.

Katie stared at the lamb. 'It's so cute!'

'That's Sherry.' Kerry stopped and gazed fondly at the lamb. 'She was our first spring baby this year.'

The lamb leaped off her mother and capered madly around the pen before skidding to a halt and staring at Katie with a wide blank gaze.

'She needs some playmates,' Kerry said. 'I think she's getting bored with just her mum for company.'

Katie thought of the long evenings she'd spent at home recently, with Mum huddled under a blanket in the corner of the sofa, staring silently at the TV. She knew how Sherry felt.

'Come on.' Kerry ducked past a bush and disappeared round a corner.

Katie followed her into a small cobbled yard. A stable block lined one side. Like the barn, its long, low roof was hump-backed. Its walls were crumbling and its wooden doors were crooked and chipped.

'They're out to pasture at the moment.' Kerry pointed past the stables to a paddock beyond.

Katie followed her gaze and saw a horse, a pony and a scruffy little donkey yanking up lumps of grass in the paddock and chewing thoughtfully. 'Does anyone ride them?'

Kerry nodded. 'Yes, people ride Swift. He's our retired racehorse. And Dusty the donkey loves giving rides to children too, though Stanley's a little too old now – he's an ancient pony!'

There was the sound of footsteps clattering on the cobbles and Katie spun round.

Asha was running toward them. 'Come and see! Come and see!' she gasped.

'What?' Kerry called. But Asha had already turned away and was charging past the paddock. Kerry and Katie began running after her.

'What's happened?' Kerry called, ducking past the bright yellow bush that leaned over the paddock fence.

Asha grinned back at them over her shoulder. 'We've found something in the duck shed.' She slowed down so that Katie could catch her up. As Kerry took the lead Asha hooked her arm through Katie's. 'And don't worry – this time it's something really good. I just *know* you're going to love it.'

# Chapter Four

'What is it?' Katie begged.

Asha shook her head. 'I can't tell you, it's a surprise.'

Kerry turned round, smiling. 'Well, at least it's good news this time.'

They followed the fence to the end of the paddock where it turned the corner and headed uphill. The path followed it, running between the paddock and another field. The path was growing steeper. Trees lined the hilltop. The city was only just visible beyond them.

'It's almost like being in the countryside,' Katie sighed.

The grass was soft underfoot. As they neared the top, Katie spotted sunlight glinting off a wide pond. Ducks waddled at the water's edge, while more ducks bobbed on the surface. The pond was fenced into a large pen.

'Did the fox get in through the fence?' Katie asked, scanning the wire fence for holes.

Asha shook her head. 'The fox only comes at night, when the ducks are in their shed.' She pointed to a wooden hut at the edge of the pen. 'The fox must have dug its way in.'

Rory and Jack were kneeling beside the shed, pushing chicken wire deep into a trench they had dug.

Rory stood up as they got to them. 'Did Asha tell you what we found?'

Kerry shook her head. 'She's being all mysterious.'

Asha opened the gate and led the way into the duck pen. 'I wanted to surprise you.' She looked up at Rory. 'Can I show Katie?'

Rory grinned and nodded. 'Of course.' Then he headed back towards Jack and picked up a spade.

Tingling with excitement, Katie followed Kerry and Asha to the shed.

It was dark inside, lit only by one small window. The floor was covered with fresh straw. Katie sneezed.

'Do you have hay fever?' Asha's thin face looked worried in the half-light.

'No. It must be because I'm not used to straw.'

Katie rubbed her itchy nose.

'You sneezed at first too, Asha,' Kerry reminded her.

'I don't any more though. And neither will you.' Asha tugged Katie's arm excitedly and led her towards the back of the barn. 'I was laying down new straw while Rory and Jack were fixing the fence and look what I found.' She knelt down and lifted up a wad of straw.

Katie peered through the gloom. She could just make out a cluster of small pale shapes. She knelt down. 'What are they?'

'Eggs!' Asha clapped her hands together.

'Duck eggs!' Katie had only ever seen hens' eggs before.

'Aren't they brilliant?' Asha touched one gently. It glowed pale as a winter sky against the straw. 'There are six of them.'

Kerry bent down over them. 'Don't let them get cold.'

Asha quickly covered the eggs with straw. 'We think they might have belonged to Quackers or Speckles.'

'Why?' Katie stood up.

'Because their mum should be sitting on them.' Asha straightened up beside her.

 43

Kerry looked thoughtful. 'Why don't you two girls stay here and see if any of the ducks come in to check the eggs?' She pointed to the far corner where shadows hid the straw. 'If you sit there quietly, the ducks won't notice you.'

'How long should we watch for?' Asha asked.

Kerry glanced at her watch. 'We can't leave it too long. Those eggs mustn't get cold.' She headed for the door. 'I'll go and have a word with Rory.'

As she disappeared, Katie followed Asha into the corner of the shed and they crouched in the shadows. Katie's gaze was fixed on the straw where the eggs were hidden.

'What if they are Speckles' or Quackers' eggs?' Katie whispered.

'*We'll* have to look after them,' Asha told her.

Katie frowned. 'But how?' The eggs were so fragile. 'Don't they have to stay at a special duck temperature.'

Asha put her arm round Katie's shoulders and gave her a squeeze. 'Don't worry. Rory will know.'

Katie fizzed with excitement. Imagine if they did have to look after the eggs! She started planning. She'd make sure they stayed safe and warm. She'd do everything Rory told her. Katie felt pride stir in her chest as she made a silent promise to Speckles and

Quackers to look after their eggs.

Suddenly, Asha stiffened beside her.

'What?' Katie looked round, alarmed.

A duck had waddled into the shed. Katie held her breath as it looked around. Perhaps they weren't going to have to nurse the eggs after all. She felt a twinge of disappointment tug at her stomach. Then the duck turned and waddled out.

'It didn't go near the eggs,' Katie gasped.

She could see Asha grinning in the darkness.

'Are you hoping to be a Mother Duck?' Asha said playfully.

Katie gave her a friendly shove. 'No,' she lied.

'It would be fun though, wouldn't it?' Asha's wide brown eyes caught Katie's.

'It would be great.' Katie's thoughts started jumping ahead. 'We could make them a nest in the barn.'

'What about when we went home?'

'We could leave a heater to keep them warm overnight.'

Asha's brow creased. 'And when they hatch?'

Katie hadn't thought about *ducklings*. Did Rory know how to look after ducklings too? She felt a pang of fear. Poor little ducklings. They had no mum and they hadn't even been born yet.

*Please let them be OK!* she silently pleaded. Katie knew all too well what it was like to suddenly feel alone in the world.

# Chapter Five

'My feet are numb,' Asha whispered.

'Mine too.' Katie realized she couldn't feel her toes. As she stretched her legs out from under her, sharp stalks of straw pricked through her jeans.

They'd been watching the eggs for half an hour now and Katie was starting to worry. No duck had come to sit on them and Kerry had gone back to the office to phone the vet. 'Do you think they're still warm enough?' she asked.

Asha began to shrug off her anorak. 'I could put my jacket over them to keep them warm.'

As she spoke, Rory popped his head round the door. 'Have any ducks been in yet?'

Asha and Katie shook their heads.

'That's it then.' Rory plucked off his woolly hat.

'We've waited long enough.' He handed his hat to Katie. 'Here you go, lass, stuff that with straw and put the eggs inside.'

Katie jumped to her feet. 'A portable nest!'

Rory looked at her and smiled. 'Exactly.' Then he took out his phone and started heading out of the shed. 'I'll phone Kerry and let her know we're bringing them back to the barn.'

Asha was already peeling the straw from the eggs.

Katie leaned in and touched one. 'It's cold!' she gasped.

'We've got to warm them up!' Asha stared at Katie, her eyes wide with alarm.

Then Katie had an idea. 'Let's fill the hat with the straw from where we were sitting.' She scrambled to the corner and began stuffing Rory's hat with the crumpled straw. It was still warm.

She held the hat out, and one at a time, Asha gently tucked the eggs into the makeshift nest.

Rory looked in through the doorway. 'Finished?'

Asha held out the hat-nest for him to see. Six pale-blue eggs poked out of the straw. 'What are we going to do with them?'

Katie took the hat and cradled it against her chest. 'The straw won't keep them warm for long.'

'Don't worry,' Rory said. 'Kerry says the vet has an incubator we can use. It will keep them at a perfect temperature until they hatch.'

Katie hugged the nest-hat closer. 'I just hope they'll be OK till then.' As she spoke, she heard a tiny cheep. She leaned down until her hair trailed over the hat.

'What's the matter?' Asha asked.

*Cheep!*

There it was again! A tiny muffled cheep.

'Did you hear a noise?' Alarmed, she rummaged through the straw, looking for cracks in the smooth blue shells.

Rory leaned closer.

*Cheep!*

A broad grin lit up his face. 'They're just letting us know they're OK.'

'It sounds like they want to get out!' Asha giggled.

'Let's not rush them,' Rory cautioned. 'They'll peck their way out when they're ready.'

Katie stroked an egg with her finger. The warm straw had already taken the chill from its shell. 'Let's get them to the barn.'

Rory nodded. 'Tuck them under your jacket, Katie, so the wind can't reach them.'

Katie folded the hat into the warmth of her anorak

and stepped out of the duck shed. After so long sitting in the gloom of the shed the sunlight felt really bright. She screwed up her eyes.

Asha tucked her arm through Katie's. 'I won't let you fall,' she said, gripping her firmly. Very carefully, Asha guided her across the duck pen and out through the gate. 'Are they OK?'

'Yes.' Katie was really glad to feel Asha's arm through hers. She was determined to get the eggs to the barn safely.

They headed down the path between the meadows. The nest-hat rustled against Katie's sweatshirt as she held it gently beneath her jacket.

As they passed the pigsty, Cynthia greeted them with a grunt.

'Sorry, Cynthia,' Asha said as they passed. 'We can't stop. We're on an important mission.'

Mud squelched under their wellies. Chickens fluttered hopefully around their legs as they crossed the yard.

'I fed you earlier,' Asha scolded, waving them away.

The chickens flapped and squabbled as they headed for the barn.

Kerry met them at the door. 'Have you got them?'

Katie nodded and opened her jacket, just enough

for Kerry to see, then slid past her into the barn. 'Where shall I put them?' She glanced around the barn for somewhere safe to put them.

'By the radiator?' Kerry offered.

Asha raced to the welly shelf and swept up an armful of abandoned scarves and gloves. 'I'll make a nest for the nest!' she said with a giggle. Scarves dangling, she raced over to the fat old radiator and, crouching, shaped the brightly coloured knitwear into a pile beside it. Then she burrowed a well in the middle and looked expectantly at Katie.

Carefully, Katie knelt down and lowered the hat into the patchwork nest. Pulling back the straw, she checked the eggs.

Kerry leaned in. 'Are they OK?'

Katie smiled. 'They're fine.' The six pale-blue eggs were still safely nestled in Rory's hat.

Asha fidgeted beside her. 'When's the vet bringing the incubator?'

Kerry looked at her watch. 'In about an hour.'

Katie could feel heat glowing from the radiator. The eggs would be warm enough till then.

Asha jumped to her feet. 'Have we got any books about hatching ducklings, Kerry?' She headed towards the bookcase beside Kerry's desk.

'I'm not sure.' Kerry followed and crouched beside Asha. As they rummaged through the books, Katie nestled deeper into the scarf-pile and gazed into the straw, listening for cheeps.

'These are all about bullying and depression and how to grow up!' Asha exclaimed. 'I *know* Harvest Hope is for unhappy kids but we still need some animal books. This is a *farm*!'

Kerry stood up. 'You're right. I'll see if I can find something in the storeroom. And while we're waiting for the vet, why don't you two muck out Billy? His pen reeks.'

Katie looked up. 'Billy?'

Asha got to her feet. 'He's one of our goats. We've got four others, Bramble, Nellie, Nancy, and Basher.'

'But what about the eggs?' Katie asked anxiously.

'I'll stay in the barn till the vet gets here,' Kerry said. 'Don't worry, I'll make sure they're all right.'

'Come on, Katie.' Asha headed for the door. 'The eggs will be OK with Kerry. And we'll be able to hear the vet's Land Rover when he arrives.'

Reluctantly, Katie stood up and followed Asha into the yard.

'We need rakes and wheelbarrows,' Asha told her, heading toward a brick shed on the far side of the yard.

As she opened the door, a spider's web billowed out into the breeze. 'Hello, Charlotte,' Asha called up to a fat black spider huddled in the corner of the door frame. 'Sorry about breaking your web.'

'Charlotte?' Katie hesitated outside the shed. She stared at the spider. It was huge.

Asha was rooting in the shadows at the back of the shed. 'She builds a new web by the door every day. It gets broken every time someone opens the door. Rory tried moving her to the window but she just went back to the door.' Metal and wood clanked as she hauled out two rakes. 'Here.' She thrust them toward Katie. 'Hold these while I grab the wheelbarrow.'

Katie grabbed the rakes, keeping one eye on Charlotte.

'She won't hurt you.' Asha grinned at her from the shadows. 'She's more scared of you than you are of her.'

'I don't think so.' Katie darted away from the door frame.

A moment later, Asha wheeled out a rusty old barrow. 'Follow me.'

She led Katie along a path that skirted the back of Cynthia's pen and headed past another vegetable plot.

'Hello, Arthur!' Asha called to an old man in frayed trousers and a torn sweater.

Arthur looked up from the raised bed he was digging. 'Hello, girls. Are you off to do some mucking out?' He pointed his spade at the barrow.

Asha grinned. 'Yep. We're mucking out Billy. Do you want the old straw for your compost heap?'

'Please!' Arthur ambled toward the fence past the rows of raised beds. They were thick with sturdy green leaves. 'Is this our new recruit?' He nodded toward Katie.

'Yes, this is Katie,' Asha told him.

'Welcome aboard, Katie.' Arthur rubbed a muddy hand on his trousers and reached over the fence. 'I'm new here too – come to help out with the gardens.'

Katie shook his hand gingerly. It felt rough and warm.

'This is where we grow our veg.' Arthur pointed to his beds. 'I'll be harvesting the last of the cabbages and leeks this week. Would you like to help later?'

Asha dropped the barrow handles. 'Yes, please!' She turned to Katie, her eyes sparkling. 'I *love* pulling up the veg. It's like magic. It's just like the stuff in the supermarket. But *we* grew it!'

'But we have to watch the eggs,' Katie reminded her.

'We can't watch them *all* the time,' Asha said. 'And they'll be safe once they're in the incubator.'

'Eggs?' Arthur's bushy eyebrows twitched. 'Incubator?'

'Asha found some duck eggs,' Katie told him. 'But it was really sad because a fox broke into the duck shed last night and took their mum. So we had to make them a nest out of a hat and some scarves and now we're looking after them.'

Arthur grinned. 'It sounds like you've had an exciting start at City Farm.'

Katie smiled back at him, suddenly happy. 'I know!'

'Just wait till the eggs hatch.' Asha started wheeling the barrow away. 'Come on, Katie. Let's get Billy mucked out before the vet gets here.'

'Got to go!' Katie called out to Arthur as she raced after her new friend.

Asha plonked the wheelbarrow down beside a wooden pen. 'That's the first time I've seen you smile,' she said.

'Is it?' Katie felt as if she'd been smiling at everyone all day.

'Well, the first time I've seen you *really* smile.' Asha took a rake from Katie. 'It's OK. We were all nervous on our first day.'

Katie wondered about Asha's first day on the Harvest Hope project. Why was she here? She seemed so happy and chatty. *Everyone* was happy and chatty at City Farm. With a stab of sadness, Katie realized how lonely she'd become at home since Mum had disappeared into her gloom.

'I'm sorry.' Asha's voice broke into Katie's thoughts. She looked really worried. 'I didn't mean to upset you.'

Katie shrugged. 'You didn't,' she said quickly. Before Asha could ask any questions she reached for the gate and unlatched it.

In the pen, hooves scrabbled on the cobbles and Katie found herself face to face with a small white goat. He had short horns and a curly beard and was staring at her with startled eyes.

'Hello,' Katie said gently. 'We've come to clean your pen.'

The goat made a soft whickering sound and began to nudge Katie's hand with his nose.

'Give him this.' Asha pushed the barrow into the pen and shut the gate behind her. Then she took a biscuit from her pocket and gave it to Katie.

Katie held it out and the goat snuffled it from her hand then gulped it down.

'Billy's so soppy.' Asha scratched him fondly between the horns, then ducked into the low shed at the end of the pen. Katie followed. There was hardly room to stand up and Katie stooped as she watched Asha begin to rake the stinky straw from the corners. She joined, working quickly. The more she raked, the more the shed stank. She wrinkled her nose and breathed through the collar of her anorak to try and block out the stench. At last, gasping, she scraped the last of the straw into a heap and heaved it out through the door. Darting after it, she took a big gulp of fresh air.

Asha staggered out after her, also gasping.

Katie laughed. 'Poor Billy! Imagine living in that smell.'

Asha reached out and patted Billy. 'He'll sleep well tonight on some nice fresh straw.' She pointed toward a low wooden block, just visible beyond the flower garden. 'We keep the straw in the stables. I'll fetch some while you rake out the pen.'

'OK.' Katie poked the old straw with her rake. 'What about this?'

'Let's load it into the barrow and I'll drop it off at the compost heap on the way.'

Katie heaved rakefuls into the barrow then, as Asha

wheeled it away, turned back to Billy. 'OK, Billy.' She spoke softly to the goat as he watched from beside his shed. 'Let's turn your pen into Buckingham Palace.'

Billy bleated.

'You don't believe me?' Katie raised her eyebrows. 'You just wait. By the time I've finished it'll be fit for a king.'

Billy followed her curiously as she worked her way round the pen, raking the old straw into the middle.

Katie paused and leaned on her rake. 'I wish Mum could see this,' she told Billy. 'She was always nagging me to clean my room. I'd love to show her your pen. My bedroom's nowhere near this bad.'

Billy lifted his head and let out a loud bleat.

'You two sound like you're getting on well.'

Katie span round as Asha parked the wheelbarrow beside the pen. 'I didn't hear you coming.'

Asha giggled. 'Too busy chatting to Billy,' she teased.

The barrow was piled high with golden straw. Asha wheeled it into the pen and Billy started tugging mouthfuls onto the ground.

'I think he wants to help…' As Katie spoke, she heard the rumble of an engine. 'Is that the vet?'

Asha froze. 'I bet it is!'

'Quick!' Katie began scattering clean straw on the ground. Asha grabbed an armful and ducked into the shed. Working fast, they emptied the barrow and reloaded it with old straw.

'Sorry, Billy.' Asha grabbed the rakes. 'We've got to go.'

Billy gave a happy bleat and wandered into his shed as Katie steered the wheelbarrow out of the pen.

Asha slid past her and raced for the barn. Katie shut the gate and hurried after her, the wheelbarrow bouncing in front of her.

'Come on!' Asha called.

As they burst into the farmyard, Katie spotted a red Land Rover.

The barn door was open and a tall man with grey hair was carrying a bright yellow, plastic box inside. Katie and Asha left the barrow and hurried inside.

By the time they got in, Rory and the tall man were lowering the yellow box onto a table beside Kerry's desk while Kerry watched.

'Katie! Asha!' Kerry waved them over. 'Come and see.'

Katie raced across the barn. 'It's not like the baby incubators you see on TV,' she said. The egg incubator looked like a cooler box, with a transparent lid.

The vet smiled at her. 'I've got a hi-tech one at the surgery, but this will do for your eggs.'

Kerry rested her hand on Katie's shoulder. 'This is Jim, Katie. He looks after the farm animals when they're sick.'

'Hi, Jim!' Asha called out cheerily.

'Hello, Asha. Nice to meet you, Katie.' Jim smiled at her. 'Do you want to see inside?' He lifted the incubator lid. The inside glowed yellow through the plastic, and the bottom was covered by a metal grille.

'Is that where the eggs will sit?' Katie stared at the grille. 'It looks very hard.'

'Eggs need plenty of ventilation as they develop.' Jim wiggled a lever on the side. 'You can use this to let in more air if the lid starts to steam up.'

Katie glanced at the eggs, still safe in Rory's hat. 'When do we put them in?'

Rory was plugging an electric cable into a wall socket. An orange light flashed on the front of the incubator.

'It'll need to warm up,' Jim told her. 'You'll know when it's at the right temperature because the light will turn green.'

Rory picked up his woolly hat with eggs in. 'First we need to mark them.'

Jim took a felt-tip pen from his pocket.

Katie frowned. 'Why?'

'The eggs need turning three times a day,' Rory explained. 'So we need to put a cross on one side and a circle on the other.'

Katie understood at once. 'So we know when they've been turned!'

Asha clasped Katie's arm. 'How did you know?'

Katie smiled and blushed.

Jim offered Katie his pen. 'Would you like to mark them?'

'Yes, please.' Katie took the pen, and as Rory held out the first egg, drew a circle on it.

Rory turned it over and Katie drew a cross on the other side. Then she watched, holding her breath, as Rory laid it gently in the incubator.

Katie handed the pen to Asha. 'You do the next one.'

Asha's eyes lit up. 'Thanks!' She took the pen and marked the next egg as Rory moved it from the hat to the incubator.

Katie and Asha took it in turns marking all the eggs carefully, until they were all safely in the incubator. Then Jim closed the lid.

Katie stared through it. 'What if they hatch in the

night, when no one's here?'

Asha gave her a squeeze. 'Don't worry, Katie. I'm sure they'll be fine. Rory gets here really early in the morning.'

Katie stared up at Rory. 'Promise you'll check the eggs first!' she begged. 'Before you do anything else.'

Rory smiled, his apple cheeks glowing. 'I promise.'

'You should have seen them, Mum! They actually cheeped inside the eggs!'

Katie was eating pizza at the kitchen table. Mum slid another slice onto her plate.

'When I go in tomorrow,' Katie chattered, 'I'm going to make a note of whether they have crosses showing or circles so I'll know when they've been turned. I wonder if Rory will let me turn them?' She stared at Mum. 'If they're making noises, does that mean they're about to hatch? What if one's hatching right now?'

Mum passed Katie some garlic bread. 'You'll find out in the morning.'

Katie glanced at her, surprised to see her mum smiling – she hadn't smiled for weeks. 'Can I go on the computer and do some research?' she asked excitedly.

'Why don't you get the laptop?' Mum suggested.

'Then you can keep me company while I bake.'

'Bake?' Katie stared at Mum, puzzled. 'Aren't you going to watch TV in the living room?' That's what Mum usually did after dinner now.

Mum stood up and started clearing the table. 'No, I'm going to make a cake.'

'A cake!' Katie smiled so widely her cheeks ached.

'We need to celebrate your eggs,' Mum said.

Katie rushed up to the study and grabbed the laptop from under the desk. When she got back to the kitchen, Mum was already measuring out sugar and butter. Katie could smell the oven warming up. She felt so happy – today had been the best day she'd had in ages. Sliding the laptop onto the table, she opened it and pressed the power button.

As Mum beat the sugar and butter into a creamy paste, Katie did a search for 'hatching duck eggs'.

'*Eggs must be turned, either automatically or by hand, a minimum of four times a day,*' Katie read from the screen. '*Lower the temperature as the eggs get closer to hatching, and open the vents more.*' She looked anxiously at Mum. 'But we don't know how close the eggs are to hatching.'

'You heard them cheep,' Mum said, as she sifted flour into a bowl.

Katie searched again. 'It says here that eggs start

making noises a few days before they hatch!' She heard Mum open the oven door. *'The eggs should cheep in response to you cheeping at them.'* Katie's heart leaped as she read from the screen. 'I can talk to them!' She read on: *'The eggs will move as the ducklings start to wriggle inside them.'*

Mum sat down beside her.

Katie pointed at the screen. 'I've found a whole forum about hatching ducklings.' Then she read something that made her sit up in shock: *'If the shells are too dry from an incubator, sometimes the shell can be too hard for them to get out.'* She turned to Mum, her eyes wide with fear. 'How will we know if the shell's too hard? What if they're trapped inside and we don't know?'

'You'll know.' Mum stroked her hair. 'I think those ducklings are in safe hands with you.'

Katie leaned her head on Mum's shoulder.

Mum gave her a squeeze. 'Keep on searching while I wash up.'

Katie heard water splash and plates clatter as Mum stood at the sink. The cake was starting to smell delicious. Life hadn't felt this normal for weeks. She scrolled though more forums.

'Would you like a piece?' Mum's voice made her look up. A big, sticky chocolate cake was sitting beside the laptop.

'What time is it?' Katie blinked in surprise. She hadn't realized how much time had passed.

Mum cut two slices and slid one over to Katie. It was lovely and warm. Katie took a bite. It was delicious.

'You're the best cake-maker in the world.' She smiled at Mum.

Mum's cheeks bulged with cake as she grinned back. 'Thanks.'

Katie sat back and let the chocolaty sponge melt over her tongue. There was only one thing that would make her feel even happier than she did right now – and that was for the eggs to hatch safely tomorrow.

# Chapter Six

Mum glanced at the dusty car keys on the hall table. Katie could see her worried frown. It had been two weeks since Mum had taken the car out.

'Don't worry,' Katie said breezily. 'I'll walk to the farm.'

Relief flooded Mum's face. 'Are you sure? I can get dressed.' She was still in her dressing gown.

'It's not far and it's sunny.' Katie was just happy that Mum had got up to make her breakfast. She wriggled into her anorak and slipped her feet into her trainers.

Mum gave her a quick kiss on the head, then headed for the stairs.

'Are you going back to bed?' Katie asked, surprised.

Mum rubbed her forehead wearily. 'Just for a little nap.'

Katie felt a stab of disappointment. She'd thought Mum was back to normal. So why was she going back to bed?

'I hope your eggs hatch,' Mum called from the stairs as Katie opened the front door.

She'd remembered the eggs – that was a good sign at least. 'I'll tell you as soon as I get home,' Katie promised.

She ran up the road and along the high street, only pausing to wait for the green man at the lights before racing the rest of the way to the farm. The sun was beaming between white, fluffy clouds. She looked at her watch. It was twenty to nine. Would Rory have checked the eggs yet? Would there be an incubator full of ducklings ready to welcome her? Katie's heart hammered in her chest as she ran under the City Farm sign and across the yard.

'Have they hatched?' she gasped as she burst into the barn.

Kerry was sat at her desk. She spun round in her chair and stared at Katie. 'Wow, you're early!'

'I wanted to see the ducklings.'

'No ducklings yet, I'm afraid.' Kerry said. 'Is your mum with you?'

'She just dropped me off. She wasn't able to stop.'

 67

Katie's face flushed – she really didn't like lying to Kerry.

'Another job interview?' Kerry asked.

Katie didn't want to lie again. 'No, she isn't feeling too good.'

'Oh, that's a shame.' Kerry looked at her sympathetically.

Katie looked away, embarrassed. 'Can I open the incubator?' she asked. 'There's something I want to try. I read about it on the internet last night.'

Kerry stood up and walked over to the incubator. 'That's sounds intriguing. But we can't leave the lid open for long.'

Katie went over to join her, nodding enthusiastically. 'I know. We have to keep the humidity and temperature constant.'

Kerry raised her eyebrows. 'I'm impressed! You *have* been doing your homework.'

The barn door burst open. 'Have they hatched?' Asha hurried in, unwinding a long pink scarf from around her neck as she crossed the barn.

Katie peered through the clear plastic. 'No, they're still eggs, but I want to try something.'

She opened the lid halfway and made a tiny cheeping sound into the incubator.

Kerry and Asha leaned in beside her.

'Listen,' Katie whispered.

Tiny cheeping noises peeped back at her.

Katie cheeped again and the eggs cheeped back. She closed the lid and grinned.

Asha's eyes were popping. 'That was magic!'

Kerry tucked a plait behind her ear. 'They recognize you!'

'It means they're nearly ready to hatch,' Katie explained.

Asha bounced up and down. 'Can we watch them in case they do?'

'Hmm, there is other work to do,' Kerry reminded her. 'The other goats need mucking out for starters.'

Asha rolled her eyes. 'But we mucked out Billy's pen yesterday.'

Kerry gave her a squeeze. 'Think how happy Bramble, Nellie, Nancy, and Basher will be to come home to fresh bedding.'

'I suppose.' Asha hooked her arm through Katie's. 'Come on then. Let's go and muck out.'

Kerry smiled. 'I'm making sandwiches for the café this morning. I'll save you some.'

A mischievous grin spread across Asha's face. 'Aren't you making any cakes today?'

Kerry frowned. 'No, I am most definitely not!'

Katie frowned, puzzled. 'What's wrong with cakes?'

'Normal cakes are great,' Asha replied. 'But Kerry's cakes are a bit' – she looked thoughtful – 'hard.'

Kerry glared at her. 'That's why I'm making sandwiches!' She tossed her plaits over her shoulder and stomped toward the kitchen.

Katie sat down on the welly bench and swapped her trainers for the red wellies she'd worn yesterday. 'Are Kerry's cakes that bad?'

'Rory threatened to call in the Healthy and Safety Inspector after her last batch.' Asha giggled and led Katie out into the yard. 'Let's get the barrow and rakes.' She headed for the tool shed.

Katie hung back while Asha opened the door and dived into the darkness. Charlotte's broken web was dangling just like yesterday. Katie scanned the door frame. 'She's gone.' She stared at the empty corner.

'Who?' Asha handed out the rakes and Katie leaned them against the shed.

'Charlotte,' Katie told her. 'She's not in her corner.'

'Perhaps she's moved house,' Asha called from inside the shed. She wheeled out the barrow and plonked it down beside Katie. 'Ooh, my neck's really itchy.'

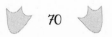

Katie saw something move on Asha's neck. It was fat and black and had long hairy legs.

*Charlotte!*

Asha brought her hand up to scratch her neck.

'No!' Katie yelled.

Asha froze. 'What's wrong'

'Stay still.' Katie gulped and reached out her hands, trying really hard to stop them from trembling.

'What?' Asha frowned. 'What is it?'

'Nothing.' Hardly breathing, Katie cupped her hands around Charlotte. She felt a tiny tickle on her palms, surprised the big spider was so light. Then she gently placed Charlotte into the shed.

Asha stared at her. 'Was that… ?' Her voice trailed away.

'Charlotte,' Katie told her. 'She was on your neck. I was scared you were going to squash her.'

Asha clasped her hands over her mouth, eyes popping. 'But I thought you were afraid of spiders.'

'So did I,' Katie said with a grin. 'But I could hardly feel her and—'

Before she could finish Asha was hugging her hard. 'You saved my life!' she squeaked.

'But I thought you liked spiders!' Katie exclaimed.

'I do, but I don't like them on me!'

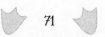

Katie struggled for breath. 'She was really gentle.'

'Thank you, thank you, thank you!' Asha finally let go of Katie and beamed. She picked up the rakes and began to head towards the goats' enclosure. As Katie grasped the wheelbarrow handles, she glanced over her shoulder and saw Charlotte scuttling up the door frame back to her web.

The other goats' pen was as bad as Billy's. It was strewn with filthy straw. Katie started work in the yard while Asha ducked in the shed. Katie raked the straw into piles, leaping out of the way when a clump of stinking straw came flying out of the shed door.

'Watch out!' she called to Asha.

'Sorry!' Asha's voice echoed from inside. She appeared in the doorway, looking hot. She unbuttoned her coat and pulled off her hat. 'It's really warm today.'

Katie stared at Asha's hair. She'd never seen her without a hat. She hadn't expected it to be so short.

As if reading her mind, Asha tugged at her fringe. 'I used to have hair that reached all the way down my back. I'm growing it again, but it's taking for ever.'

'Why did you have it cut?' Katie liked her own shoulder-length bob, but she'd always imagined how nice it would be to have really long hair.

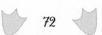

'The treatment made it all fall out.'

'Treatment?'

Asha looked surprised. 'I'm sorry. I keep forgetting not everyone knows I had leukaemia.' She slipped off her jacket and hung it on a fence post. 'When I was ill, everyone made such a fuss, I thought the whole world must know. Plus I got all skinny and sick-looking. Mum's been feeding me up since I went into remission.'

'Does that mean you're cured?' Katie had never met anyone who'd had leukaemia but she knew it was really serious.

'Yep.' Asha pushed at the straw with her rake absent-mindedly. 'But I have regular check-ups, just in case.'

Katie was bursting with questions. What was it like to be so ill? Was she scared? Why did she need regular check-ups if she was better? But she wasn't sure whether Asha would want to talk about it. 'Did it hurt?' she asked cautiously.

'It made me feel really poorly,' Asha said, looking down at the ground. 'But I love being healthy again. I never used to notice how brilliant it feels to wake up full of energy and to be able to do anything I want without getting tired or sick.'

'So that's why you're on the Harvest Hope project?' Katie guessed.

Asha nodded. 'My doctors thought the fresh air would do me good. But it's made me feel better in so many other ways.' She looked at Katie. 'Why are you here? Kerry just said you'd been off school a lot. She didn't tell us why. Have you been ill too?'

Katie gripped her rake. She could feel herself flushing. 'I – I—' She didn't know what to say. It wasn't her that was ill, it was Mum. For a moment Katie felt really bad for being there. Her place could have been given to another girl like Asha, who really was ill. Not someone who missed school because her mum was too sad to get out of bed. A dark guilty feeling sat like a stone in Katie's stomach.

'Asha! Katie!' Rory's voice sounded from the yard. 'Quick! They're hatching!'

Asha dropped her rake and raced for the gate. 'Come on, Katie!'

Katie dashed after her. Rory was standing at the barn door. He held it open as they rushed past him and scrambled inside.

Kerry was standing next to the incubator. Quietly, she put a finger to her lips. Katie tiptoed across the barn and peered inside the incubator.

The lid was open and two of the eggs were rocking. Cheeping noises sounded from inside and Katie could hear tapping.

'They're pecking their way out. I read about this last night on the internet.' Katie grabbed Asha's arm. They both stared into the incubator, as still as statues. It felt like they'd been standing there for ages. Eventually, a tiny piece of shell broke off one of the eggs, then another. The tapping grew louder and louder until, finally, the first egg cracked.

Katie felt really nervous. Should they help? What if the shell was too hard? What if the duckling couldn't get out? The end of the egg split open and an orange bill poked out. Everyone peered over the incubator, watching as the little baby bird struggled to break free. Then, very slowly, the bedraggled duckling began to drag itself from the shell.

Katie was amazed how big it was. 'It must have been so squished in there!'

'Can we pull the rest of the shell off?' Asha asked, as the duckling fought to escape.

Rory shook his head. 'No, lass, it'll find its own way out.'

Kerry's beads clicked softly as she leaned over the incubator. 'This is wonderful,' she sighed.

Another egg wobbled, then split, and a second round orange beak appeared.

'Are they all going to hatch today?' Katie asked excitedly. The rest of the eggs were moving, but only gently.

'It may take another day or two,' Rory told her.

Katie leaned closer and made a cheeping noise. The four eggs cheeped back at her.

Rory let out a laugh. 'Where did you learn that?'

'On the internet,' Katie told him.

Asha grinned. 'At least we know they're all alive.'

'And two have hatched.' Katie's heart swelled with joy as the two ducklings shook off their shells and struggled to their feet. They tottered for a second, then fell over again.

'Is there something wrong?' she asked anxiously. 'Why can't they stand up?'

'Don't worry about that,' Rory reassured them. 'The poor little things are just worn out from hatching. We'd better close the lid,' he added. 'They'll be feeling the cold.'

Katie wanted to watch and watch until every duckling had hatched, but she knew the chicks needed warmth. She stood back as Rory closed the lid.

'I can still see them.' Asha peered through the clear

plastic. 'They're so cute!'

The yellow ducklings waddled across the metal grille and huddled together in a corner.

'We have to make them somewhere soft to nest!' Katie exclaimed.

Asha quickly scanned the barn. 'Can we use that box?' She pointed to a cardboard box sitting on top of a cupboard.

Kerry looked thoughtful. 'It's got the painting trays in it.' Her face brightened. 'Wait, I've got an idea.' She dashed toward the café.

Katie glanced toward the radiator where they'd made the first duck nest. They couldn't keep the ducklings there. With people coming and going, it would be noisy and scary. They needed to be out of the way but it had to be somewhere warm. She looked at the stove. Logs were glowing inside.

'We could keep the ducklings there.' She pointed to the space beside the stove. 'They'd be warm and cosy and out of the way.'

'And we could see them from the sofas,' Asha added.

Rory rubbed his chin. 'They certainly would be cosy there,' he agreed. 'But they have to stay in the incubator until tomorrow.'

'That's OK.' Katie was already heaving one of the

sofas away from the stove to make more room for the nest. 'That gives us loads of time to get it ready for them.'

As she spoke, Kerry appeared from the café kitchen holding a large cardboard box. 'One of the delivery men left this earlier.'

'That's perfect!' Asha took the box from her and put it on the floor near the stove. 'We can line it with newspaper and straw.'

'Yesterday's newspaper is on my desk,' Kerry told her.

'I'll fetch it.' Katie dashed to Kerry's desk and snatched up the paper.

'I'll get straw! Come on, Rory! You can help me.' Asha raced out of the barn, dragging Rory after her.

Katie began to line the bottom of the box with the newspaper. 'What do ducklings eat?' she called over her shoulder to Kerry.

'The vet left some feed that we can mix with water,' Kerry answered. 'And I've ordered some corn meal. He said we can make it into a mash for them. But he did say they'd need quite a varied diet so we'll need to do some more research.'

'I'll check the internet when I get home.' Katie tingled with excitement as she thought about making

78

all sorts of tasty meals for the ducklings.

Asha burst into the barn, trailing armfuls of straw. She dropped it beside Katie. 'I'll clean up the mess,' she said, looking back at the scattered stalks.

But Rory was already following, picking them up. 'You make the nest,' he told her. 'Make sure you cover any cracks in the box well. Those ducklings won't like draughts.'

'Thanks, Rory.' Asha knelt beside Katie and together they began carefully laying the straw in the box, pressing it into the edges and corners to make sure the nest was snug and warm.

Katie was concentrating so hard that she jumped with surprise when, ten minutes later, a tray clattered onto the coffee table behind them.

She glanced over her shoulder.

Kerry was arranging biscuits on a plate while four mugs steamed beside it. 'Go and wash your hands,' she said with a smile. 'I've made us all some hot chocolate.'

'Hot chocolate!' Asha leaped to her feet and sprinted for the hand basin. Katie followed, reaching the sink just in time to catch the soap as it flew from Asha's hands.

'Kerry makes the best hot chocolate,' she grinned.

'Better than her cakes?' Katie whispered.

'Much better.' Asha held her soapy hands under the tap. 'She puts marshmallows in it and everything!'

'Mmmm.' Katie rinsed her hands happily and headed for the sofas where Rory and Kerry were already sunk into the deep cushions.

Katie curled onto the next sofa, ducking as Asha leaped in next to her. 'Where's Jack today?' Asha asked.

'Out with his mum and grandad,' Kerry told her. 'He'll be back tomorrow.'

Asha leaned forward and grabbed a mug of hot chocolate. 'He'll be so surprised when he sees the ducklings.' She passed the mug to Katie and reached for another.

Katie took it gratefully. The busy morning had made her starving hungry. When Kerry offered her the biscuit plate, she was quite relieved to see that they weren't home-made. 'Is it OK if I have two?'

'You can have as many as you want.' Kerry's gaze slid sideways to Asha who had taken a handful. 'Farming is clearly hungry work.'

Asha looked up with a cheeky grin. 'You know I'm meant to be eating lots.'

Rory stretched back in the sofa and rested his mug

of cocoa on his belly. 'You eat more grub than Swift,' he teased.

'Swift's our racehorse,' Asha explained to Katie.

Katie nodded, her mouth full of biscuit. She remembered seeing him in the paddock yesterday.

Asha slurped from her mug, then looked at Kerry, her lips frothy with cocoa foam. 'This is your best hot chocolate ever, Kerry.'

Katie tasted hers. It was sweet and perfectly chocolaty. 'It's yummy!'

Kerry grinned. 'Well, at least there's one yummy thing I can make for the café!'

# Chapter Seven

The farmyard was really quiet as Katie headed for the barn the next morning. There weren't even any chickens squabbling and pecking at the ground. Catching her breath, Katie checked her watch.

*Eight-fifteen.*

She'd left home early and run all the way because she wanted to see if the other ducklings had hatched. But maybe she'd left a bit too early. Was she the first one here?

She turned the handle of the barn door, half expecting it to be locked. She was relieved when it opened.

'Hello, lass!' Rory's voice surprised her. He was sitting on the welly bench pulling on his big black boots. 'Looks like someone got up with the lark this

 82

morning.'

'Yeah,' Katie gasped, trying to get her breath back.

'Have you been running?'

'Yes! All the way here.'

'Your mum didn't bring you?'

Katie's heart began to pound. 'She's not very well, and it isn't far.' Katie turned to the incubator so he wouldn't see her blushing. 'Have the other ducklings hatched?'

Rory nodded. 'Go and have a look.'

Excited, Katie ran to the incubator and lifted the lid. Six brown and yellow ducklings were huddled in the corner. Their shells lay broken on the wire mesh. 'They're all fluffy!' Katie couldn't believe how cute they were now that their feathers had dried. 'They must have hatched in the night.' She straightened, suddenly worried. 'They must be starving.'

Rory crossed the room and came to stand next to her. 'I'll make them some corn meal mash when we move them to their new nest.' He glanced at the box Asha and Katie had prepared yesterday.

'Can we do it now?' Katie asked. Then she paused. 'Actually, let's wait for Asha. She'll want to help.'

'And Jack will be back today,' Rory reminded her.

Katie grinned. 'He's not seen any of the ducklings.

I can't wait to show him.'

'They won't be here till nine,' Rory told her. 'Why don't you help me take Swift out to pasture while we wait?'

'The racehorse?' Katie bubbled with excitement. 'Yes, please!'

'Get your wellies on, then.' Rory shut the lid of the incubator.

As Katie pulled on her red wellies, she noticed Rory watching her. He looked thoughtful, as though something was worrying him. 'Is something wrong with the ducklings?' she asked anxiously.

'The *ducklings* are fine.' Rory reached under his woolly hat and scratched his head. 'Come on, then. Swift will be wanting a gallop.'

Katie followed him to the stables and waited while he unlatched Swift's door. The old racehorse was so much bigger up close.

Rory unhooked a head collar while Swift scuffed his hooves impatiently in the straw. Rory hooked the head collar over the horse's huge head, then led him into the cobbled yard. 'Will you hold him while I let Stanley out?' Rory held out the lead rope.

Katie took it gingerly.

'Don't worry, he's gentle as a lamb in the yard.'

Rory patted Swift's neck.

Katie looked up at Swift, her fingers clutching tightly to the rope. What if he made a sudden dash for the paddock? He was eyeing it, tail swishing, as though he could hardly wait to be cantering along the soft grass.

Hooves clopped on the cobbles and Katie saw Rory leading out a black and white pony.

'You take Stanley.' Rory took Swift's lead rope and gave her Stanley's. 'Swift can pull a bit when we get near the paddock.'

Katie took Stanley's rope gratefully. The pony's spine was sunken with age and his eyes didn't shine like Swift's but he whickered at Katie and nudged her shoulder with his white-flecked nose. Rory set off toward the field and Katie followed, tugging gently on Stanley's lead rope. The old pony trotted beside her. Katie could feel the warmth of his flank through the crisp morning air.

'It's going to be a sunny day,' Rory said, looking at the clear sky. He paused as they reached the paddock gate and looked down at Katie. 'It's good to see you here so early. I wasn't sure you were going to turn up every day, to be honest.'

Katie looked at him, puzzled. 'Really?'

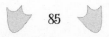

'Kerry told me you'd been off sick from school quite a lot recently.' Rory unhooked the latch. 'I thought maybe you'd be sick here too.'

'Oh!' Katie finally understood what he meant. 'No, it's OK, I can walk here by myself,' she explained. 'School's further away so I can't get there unless Mum drives me.'

Rory swung open the gate and she led Stanley through.

'How do I take off his head collar?'

Rory didn't seem to hear. He was frowning.

'Rory?'

'What's that, lass?'

'How do I undo Stanley's head collar?'

'Like this.' Rory unbuckled a strap and drew it gently over the pony's ears. Stanley sniffed at Katie's hair, his warm breath tickling her ear, then plodded off towards a lush clump of grass and began grazing.

As Stanley wandered away, Rory released Swift and he leaped away with a whinny and galloped across the field to join Dusty at the far side.

'Katie!'

Katie spun around to see Asha hanging over the fence. 'Have you seen the ducklings?'

Katie waved excitedly. 'Yes!'

Jack came running along the paddock fence. 'They've all hatched!'

Katie turned to Rory. 'Can we put them in their new nest now?'

Rory grinned. 'Yes, I think you'd better!'

As Katie went to join Asha, Jack skidded to a stop beside them. 'I can't believe they hatched already,' he panted. 'I was only away for one day.'

'They're so fluffy and cute!' Asha beamed.

'Rory said we can put them in their nest box,' Katie told them.

'Let's tell Kerry!' Asha started racing off towards the barn. Jack tore after her with Katie sprinting at his heels.

Jack reached the barn first. As he burst through the door, Asha waited for Katie to catch up.

'We need to give them names,' she said, panting for breath.

'I was trying to think of names last night in bed,' Katie told her, as they followed Jack inside.

'Should we call one *Quackers the Second*?' Asha asked.

'It's a bit long,' Katie said.

'Wow, you're all in early today.' Kerry called out across the barn. She was standing by the incubator, peering through the lid.

'We wanted to see the ducklings.' Katie hurried to join her.

'We've been thinking up names,' Asha told her.

Jack leaned in beside them. 'Can we call one "Wolverine"?'

'Wolverine?' Kerry raised her eyebrows.

'Why not?' Jack asked.

Boots clumped across the barn and Katie turned and saw Rory heading toward them.

'Let's get these ducklings into their new home,' he said.

Asha rushed over to the cardboard box beside the stove and peered in. 'It looks so nice and cosy.' She reached down and felt inside. 'And it's warm.'

'Let's keep it that way.' Kerry glanced at the stove. 'That fire will need stoking up,' she said. 'I'll fetch some logs.'

As Kerry headed outside, Rory opened the lid of the incubator. The ducklings were snuggled together, cheeping. Their orange bills opened and closed eagerly.

'I think they're hungry,' Katie said.

'They'll get their breakfast soon enough. Let's settle them into their new home first.' Rory reached into the incubator and cupped a duckling in his hands.

Holding it gently, he carried it over to the box and put it down in the straw. 'Do you think you can do the next one, Katie?'

'I think so.' Holding her breath, Katie reached into the incubator. The ducklings scattered and she froze, wondering what to do.

'Just move your hands slowly toward one,' Rory told her.

Katie reached for one of the ducklings, and closed her hands around it quickly. It was like catching Charlotte the spider, but it wriggled more fiercely. Very carefully, she lifted it out of the incubator.

The duckling squirmed in her hands. It was so soft she could hardly feel its feathers. But she could feel its wings flapping and its feet scrabbling against her fingers. 'It's so strong!' She was surprised that such a tiny creature could kick so hard. She carried the duckling over to the box, then leaned down and dropped it carefully into the straw.

Peeping, it scurried toward its nest-mate and they huddled together.

Katie moved out of the way as Asha headed toward the box, with another duckling in her hands. Jack followed with a fourth and Katie raced back to the incubator, eager to carry another one.

She scooped up a duckling easily this time. It wriggled in her hands and she held it for a few moments longer before plopping it into the box. She wanted to feel its feet and feathers against her fingers.

Asha arrived with the last duckling. 'They're so sweet,' she cooed as she released it beside its brothers and sisters.

Behind them, water drummed in the sink. Rory was filling a paint tray under the tap.

He carried it carefully to the nest and put it inside. The ducks waddled round it, cheeping. Then one clambered over the side and splashed down into the water. In a rush, the others followed, wading in the shallows and flicking droplets as they stretched and flapped their wings.

Katie watched them, grinning. 'When will they be ready for a proper swim?'

'A week or two, I reckon,' Rory answered.

The barn door swung open and Kerry staggered in, her arms laden with logs. Jack rushed to help her, lifting logs from her pile and carrying them to the stove. He stacked them on the hearth and used the tongs to open the stove door.

'Thanks, Jack.' Kerry held her load out and Jack took another log and pushed it into the stove.

90

'Shall I put another one in?' he asked.

Kerry looked at the glowing embers and nodded. 'A couple of small ones, to get it going.' She glanced at the ducklings splashing in the box. 'We don't want our little babies getting cold.'

Asha rested her chin on the edge of the box. 'I'm going to call one of them Baby,' she sighed.

Jack rolled his eyes. 'They can't have soppy names!'

Asha stared at him. 'Why not?'

'They're ducks, not people,' Jack said. 'The need proper duck names.'

'What, like *Wolverine*?' Asha stood up.

Kerry dropped her pile of logs onto the hearth. 'I could hear a lot of hungry bleating while I was fetching wood.' She closed the stove door. 'The animals need feeding.'

'I'll help.' Jack reached for his wellies.

'Me too.' Asha grabbed hers from under the bench.

'Can I stay here?' Katie didn't want to leave the ducklings. They might be frightened in their new nest. Or lonely. She hooked her chin over the edge of the box and cheeped. Six bills turned toward her and cheeped back.

Kerry smiled. 'I think you'd better, seeing as you speak their language!'

As Katie cheeped again and the ducklings cheeped back, Rory appeared from the café, a bowl in his hands. 'They seem to recognize your quack,' he chuckled. 'They must think you're their mum.' He handed Katie a plate of mushy duck food.

'If they think I'm their mum then I've *got* to stay with them,' Katie said firmly and placed the bowl in the box.

The ducklings scrambled out of the paint tray and pressed around the bowl, jostling each other to reach the food.

Asha pulled on her wellies. 'Are you sure you don't want to come with us?' she asked. 'When we've finished feeding, we're cleaning out the guinea pigs. You haven't met Bubble and Squeak yet. They're even cuter than the ducklings.'

'They can't be.' Katie gazed lovingly into the box. The ducklings had settled around the bowl and were scooping up mouthfuls of mush with their bills, swallowing greedily.

Jack peered over her shoulder. 'Just make sure Wolverine gets his fair share,' he said. 'He looks hungry.'

Katie looked up at Jack. 'How do you know which is which?'

92

'Wolverine's got a v-shape of brown feathers on his head.' He pointed to the tiniest duck.

Katie blinked in surprise. As she looked harder she found each duckling had a different pattern of brown feathers among the yellow. As Asha and Jack followed Rory out of the barn, she started memorizing each fluffy coat.

'Katie!'

Kerry's call made Katie jump. She'd been watching the ducklings all day. She'd only stopped once, when Kerry had brought sandwiches from the cafe for lunch.

'Katie?' Kerry called again.

'Maybe you should try quacking at her.' Rory was resting on a sofa, warming his toes in front of the stove.

Katie stood up and stretched. 'I think I can recognize them all now.' Earlier in the day she'd named the ducklings. She'd kept the names Asha and Jack had wanted – Baby and Wolverine were the easiest to tell apart; Wolverine was the smallest, Baby was the biggest. The others – Buttercup, Waddles, Charlie and Scruffy – had their own personalities already. Waddles kept tripping over, and Scruffy's feathers stuck out messily. Buttercup stayed close to the food bowl while Charlie tried to keep the miniature paint-tray pond to himself, cheeping crossly at the others if they climbed in.

'What time is it?' Katie suddenly realized that Jack and Asha had left quite a while ago. She looked up and her heart sank. It was dark outside!

Kerry looked at her watch. 'What time did your mum say she was picking you up?'

Rory sat up straight on the sofa and looked at Katie. 'She is coming to pick you up, isn't she?'

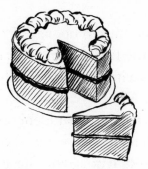

# Chapter Eight

Katie stared at Rory. 'Sh-she's poorly,' she stammered. 'I was going to walk home.'

Rory and Kerry exchanged glances.

'Well, it's too dark for you to walk now.' Kerry picked up her keys from her desk. 'I'll drive you home.'

Katie froze. She couldn't say no. It *was* too dark. But what if Mum was still in bed when they arrived?

'Come on, Katie.' Kerry jangled her car keys.

Stiff with worry, Katie unhooked her coat from its peg. Perhaps Mum would be dressed. She might even be baking again. Maybe Kerry would drop her at the gate instead of coming in.

Rory stood and stretched. 'I'll lock up here, Kerry,' he said with a yawn.

Katie slipped on her coat and huddled inside it as

 95

she followed Kerry out to her car.

'How are the ducklings doing?' Kerry asked, as she pulled out of the car park.

'They're fine.' Katie shrank beneath the seat belt.

'Which way do I go here?' Kerry asked as they reached the high street.

'Left. My road's on the right.' Katie closed her eyes and wished. *Please let Mum be cooking tea and dressed and acting happy.*

'Which turning is your road?' Kerry asked.

Reluctantly, Katie answered. 'The one after the pet shop.'

Kerry flicked on the indicator. It ticked as loud as a bomb. 'Tell me when we get to your house. It's number fifty-three, isn't it?'

The car bumped over the speed humps.

'It's just here.' Katie pointed to her house as came into view, her chest tightening as Kerry pulled up outside.

Katie breathed a tiny sigh of relief. The downstairs lights were on.

*Please let her be dressed.*

But the curtains were still open, not shut against the cold and dark like the other houses.

*Perhaps Mum had been too busy baking.*

Kerry got out of the car and shut the door.

Katie unclicked her seat belt and got out too. She unlatched the garden gate and led Kerry up the path. On the doorstep, she fumbled in her pocket for her door key. Mum had given it to her a few weeks ago so she didn't have to get out of bed to let her in.

She opened the front door. 'Mum?'

The house felt chilly. Katie switched on the hall light.

'Mum?'

'Katie!' Mum appeared at the bright kitchen doorway. 'I was getting really worried – why are you so late?' She was in her pyjamas and dressing gown, but at least she was out of bed. 'I came down to put the heating on.' She rubbed her arms. 'It's chilly tonight—' She broke off as Kerry appeared though the front door behind Katie.

'Hello, I'm Kerry,' Kerry said brightly. 'I hope you don't mind me popping in. I gave Katie a lift home and I thought I should say hello.'

Mum wrapped her dressing gown tighter round her. 'H-hello, I'm Bea,' she stammered.

'Sorry, Mum,' Katie said quickly. 'It got too dark to walk. I didn't realize it was so late.'

Mum looked at Kerry, embarrassed. 'Sorry, I

haven't been feeling too well. I—'

'Yes, Katie said you'd been a bit poorly,' Kerry said with a broad smile.

Mum smiled back, her cheeks flushing. 'Well, thanks for bringing her home, Kerry.' She stepped forward and shook Kerry's hand. 'It's lovely to meet you. Katie's talked a lot about you and Rory. And the ducklings, of course.'

Kerry grinned. 'I don't know what those ducklings would have done without her. She hasn't taken her eyes off them all day.'

'They've all hatched?' Mum tucked her hair behind her ear.

Katie blinked. She'd forgotten Mum didn't know yet! 'The rest of them hatched in the night.' She grinned. 'We put them in their nest-box this morning. I've named them all.'

'Have you?' Mum sounded surprised.

'Wolverine, Baby, Charlie, Waddles, Scruffy and Buttercup,' Katie told her proudly.

Mum laughed. 'How on earth do you tell them apart?'

'It's easy once you get to know them.' Katie shrugged off her coat.

Mum turned toward the kitchen. 'Would you like a

cup of coffee, Kerry.'

Katie stiffened. Kerry mustn't stay. She might find out how sad Mum had been. Mum sounded happy now, but what if her mood suddenly changed? Katie knew that just one wrong word could make her sad again.

'That would be lovely.'

Katie's heart sank as Kerry accepted Mum's invitation.

'Go and get the chocolate cake down from the cupboard,' Mum told Katie.

Kerry's eyes lit up. 'Chocolate cake?'

Mum nodded. 'It's a couple of days old, but that's the great thing about chocolate cake. If you keep it airtight, the flavour improves.'

'I'd have to keep mine airtight for a year,' Kerry laughed. 'I'm not very good at baking.' She followed Mum into the kitchen.

Katie squeezed round them and pulled the cake tin from the cupboard. Mum put the kettle on and fetched plates. She cut three slices of the chocolate cake while Kerry sat at the kitchen table and slid off her coat.

Mum handed Kerry a slice of cake and then went back to the kettle to make the drinks.

'Oh my goodness!' Kerry exclaimed.

Katie's heart flipped in her chest. 'What?'

Kerry's mouth was full of cake. She swallowed quickly. 'This cake is *delicious*! So moist and chocolaty. You're a lucky girl, Katie, having a mum who can bake like this!'

Relief swamped Katie. 'I know.' She gave Mum a quick hug.

'Would it be OK if I just had a quick word with your mum?' Kerry said, looking at Katie.

Katie stood rooted to the spot. What if Mum said the wrong thing? If she left her on her own with Kerry she wouldn't be able to cover any slip-ups. She looked at Mum questioningly. Mum gave a her a little nod and passed her a slice of cake.

'Here you go, love. Why don't you take this up to your bedroom while I have a chat with Kerry?'

Katie took the cake and reluctantly left the kitchen. When she got to her bedroom she flicked on the light and put her cake on the bedside table. Then she perched on the edge of her bed and clenched her hands together. She could hear the murmur of voices downstairs. What did Kerry want to talk about? Was she going to ask Mum lots of questions? Katie chewed at her thumbnail. She'd told all those lies at the farm, about her mum being poorly and having job interviews. She'd tried so hard not to give Mum away. But now it could all go wrong. Her head began to swim.

She began swinging her legs against the side of her bed, unable to sit still. If Kerry found out it was Mum who was unwell, not Katie, she might stop her visiting the farm. Katie nibbled harder at her thumbnail. She'd never see Asha again.

*Or the ducklings!*

Katie gasped.

Who'd look after them?

Her heart began to race. Hours seemed to pass, though the clock only showed twenty minutes had gone by before Mum called up the stairs.

'Kerry's leaving! Come and say goodbye.'

Katie raced to the head of the stairs and stared down at Kerry, trying to read her expression. Had she found out about the lies? Was she going to tell her that she couldn't come to the farm any more?

Kerry waved. 'Bye, Katie!' she called. 'Thanks for letting me bring you home. I've never tasted such good cake.' She held out a piece wrapped in clingfilm. 'Your mum's given me some to take home. I hope you don't mind.'

Katie ventured down a few steps. 'No, that's OK.'

'Great.' Kerry turned toward the door. 'See you at the farm tomorrow.'

'Yes, see you,' Katie echoed, limp with relief.

As Kerry left, Katie felt like leaping up and down with relief. She was going back to the farm. She was going to see the ducklings again.

# Chapter Nine

Just as Katie finished getting dressed she smelled toast. She galloped downstairs, her hair wet from her morning shower, and swung round the kitchen door. 'Mum?'

Mum was at the table buttering toast. She looked up with a smile. 'Good morning, love.'

Katie blinked in surprise. Mum was dressed, her hair brushed and the dark circles under her eyes hidden beneath make-up. 'You look really pretty!'

'Thank you.' Mum nibbled at her bottom lip like she always did when she was nervous. 'Can I come to the farm with you this morning?'

'Of course!' Katie slid into her chair, wondering if she was dreaming.

'I want to see those ducklings I've heard so much

about.' Mum handed her a slice of toast.

'I can't wait for you to see them!' Katie said, as Mum started emptying the dishwasher. 'You can hold one if you like.'

Mum clattered plates into the cupboard. 'Do they bite?'

Katie laughed. 'They nibble a bit but their bills are just tickly.'

'Bills,' Mum echoed, her gaze falling upon the pile of unopened brown envelopes in the corner of the kitchen.

Katie sighed. Why hadn't she said 'beaks'? Now Mum would be worrying about all the bills she had to pay, but wasn't able to because she didn't have enough money. 'Charlie's my favourite,' she said quickly. 'He's definitely the cutest. But don't tell the other ducklings I said that.'

'Eat your toast.' Mum sounded distracted. 'We don't want to be late.'

Katie took a bite of her toast, but she didn't really feel hungry any more.

The wind was warm on Katie's face as they headed out of the gate.

'Shall we walk to the farm?' Mum suggested. 'The

104

fresh air will do us good.'

'OK.' Katie unzipped her jacket, hot already in the sunshine.

'How did you know which way to go on your first day?' Mum asked, as Katie led her along the high street.

'I remembered passing the farm in the car,' Katie told her.

Mum glanced warily at the factories as they turned up the road for City Farm. 'It's not very pretty.'

'Wait till you get to the farm,' Katie said excitedly. 'It's like a magic secret world.'

A lorry rumbled past.

'I should have driven you.' Mum started looking really sad, like she was about to cry. 'I can't believe I let you walk all this way by yourself.'

'It's fine, Mum,' Katie said. 'I like walking.' She didn't add that she'd enjoyed the feeling of independence. She'd felt more grown up each time she visited the farm. Instead, she grasped Mum's hand and tugged her faster along the pavement.

As she led Mum under the City Farm sign, Katie heard bleating. 'That's Billy the goat,' she told Mum. 'I bet he can hear the feed bucket rattling.'

Chickens swarmed at their feet as they crossed the yard.

Mum froze and pulled Katie close. 'Oh no! Have they escaped?'

Katie laughed and struggled free. 'It's OK, Mum. They're meant to be here.' She shooed the chickens away with a wave of her arms. 'They're just hoping that we'll feed them.'

'Katie!' Jack came out of the tool shed, pushing a wheelbarrow.

'There's Jack.' Katie waved at him. 'How's Charlotte?'

Jack looked up at the corner of the door frame. 'She's fine.'

'Charlotte?' Mum looked puzzled.

'She's the spider who lives in the tool shed. Come on, follow me.' Katie pushed open the barn door.

Asha was kneeling beside the ducklings' box.

'Hi, Asha,' Katie called.

Asha jumped to her feet. 'I've been playing with Baby!' She raced across the barn and gave Katie a hug. She pulled away and glanced at Katie's mum.

'Hello.' Mum smiled. 'Are you Asha?'

Asha nodded enthusiastically. 'Are you Katie's mum?'

'Yes. Call me Bea.' Mum ruffled Katie's hair. Katie felt aglow with happiness.

106

Kerry appeared in the café archway. Her purple blouse was powdered with flour and a frown furrowed her forehead.

Asha leaned close to Katie. 'Kerry's been baking again,' she hissed.

'Uh-oh,' Katie whispered back with a grin.

'Hello, Bea.' Kerry wiped her hand on the side of her skirt and held it out as she crossed the barn. 'I'm so glad you decided to come.'

Mum shook her hand. 'Me too,' she said with a smile.

'Come and see the ducklings!' Katie said, tugging her over to the nest-box. 'Watch this!' She leaned over the box and made a soft cheeping sound. Instantly, six orange bills turned toward her and began cheeping madly.

'Oh, how cute!' Mum exclaimed.

'They only cheep for Katie,' Asha told her. 'I've been trying since I got here this morning but they just ignore me.' She called to the ducklings from the other side of the box, but they crowded towards Katie, falling over each other to get closest.

'Their mash bowl is empty,' Katie said. 'Has anyone fed them yet?'

'Rory gave them breakfast before he went to feed

the other animals,' Kerry told her. 'He said they'll need another meal at eleven o'clock. Can you do that, Katie? He left the bag of duck food in the kitchen.'

'Sure.' Katie leaned into the box. 'It's OK, duckies. I'll feed you again soon.'

The ducks tried to scramble up the inside of the box, climbing onto each other's backs to be nearer to her.

Mum crouched beside Katie and gave her a squeeze. 'So, who's who?'

Proudly, Katie pointed to each duck in turn. 'Wolverine, Charlie, Waddles, Scruffy and Buttercup.'

Asha looked in. 'Where's Baby? I can't tell which is which when they're all squished up together.'

'That one.' Katie pointed to the biggest duckling.

Asha squinted and shook her head. 'I still can't tell.'

'I'll show you.' Katie turned to Kerry. 'Can I lift one out?'

'Yes, but be careful.' Kerry hurried back toward the café where a timer was beeping.

Katie reached into the box and lifted Baby out. The duckling felt warm in her hands. Its feathers brushed softly against her fingers. Cupping it gently, she held it out for Asha to see. 'See, it's got two stripes on its head. And three on each wing.'

'I can't see her wings.' Asha pulled at Katie's fingers, trying to see more.

'Let me put the duckling down so you can have a good look.'

Mum moved away so there was a space on the carpet. 'Won't she run away?'

'I can catch it if it does,' Katie said. She crouched and plopped Baby onto the floor.

The duckling froze, staring about with round, black eyes.

Asha knelt down beside it. 'She's so pretty!'

'We don't know if it's a girl or a boy yet.' At the sound of Katie's voice, Baby turned and raced toward her, cheeping excitedly.

'She loves you!' Mum gasped.

Asha waved Katie backwards. 'Try walking! See if she follows you.'

'What if she runs under one of the sofas?' Mum looked worried. 'You won't be able to reach her.'

'It's OK. I saw some people doing this on the internet. Baby will come out for food.' Katie took a step away from the duckling and it hurried after her, cheeping. Katie felt a rush of delight. She could hear the other ducklings calling from the box. They were scrabbling desperately against the side.

'Let's get another one out!' Asha lifted another duckling out of the box. She put it on the carpet. 'Try calling it!'

Katie recognized the duckling's messy feathers immediately. 'Scruffy!' she sang.

Scruffy looked up and ran, cheeping, towards Katie.

Asha lifted another from the box, then another, until all the ducklings were clustered on the carpet.

'Duckies!' Katie called, backing away.

In a bunch, they hurried toward her. Katie giggled as they crowded at her feet.

Laughing, Mum sat on a sofa and pulled her feet up out of the way as Katie began to parade around it. The ducklings scurried after her like a tiny train.

Asha clapped her hands together with joy.

Suddenly, the door opened. A breeze billowed into the barn as Rory stood in the doorway.

Alarmed, Katie spun round. 'Quick! Close the door!'

'How did the ducks escape?' Rory asked, raising his bushy white eyebrows in surprise.

'They didn't escape,' Asha explained. 'Katie's taking them for a walk. Go on, Katie. Show Rory.'

Katie paced across the barn. Behind her, the ducks tumbled over each other as they tried to be closest.

'I've heard of a mother hen, and Mother Goose,' Rory chuckled. 'But never a mother duck.'

Katie led the ducklings back to their nest-box. 'I don't want them getting cold.' She crouched and began to lift them one by one back into the box.

Mum watched, eyes glistening. 'You're a natural mother.'

Katie nudged Wolverine gently into the paint tray so he could splash about in the shallows. 'They're just so cute,' she sighed, as the others clambered in after him and began squabbling for space.

Rory cleared his throat and walked over to Mum. 'Hello. I'm guessing you must be this young lady's mum?'

Mum stood up. 'Yes. I'm Bea.'

'Very pleased to meet you.' Rory tugged off his hat.

Mum smiled, as his curly white hair burst like springs from the top of his head. 'You must be Rory.'

Rory smoothed his hair with his hand 'Aye. So, has Katie been telling you all about the farm?'

'Oh, yes,' Mum said. 'She's talked about nothing else. Especially the ducklings.'

'Katie and the ducklings have certainly taken to each other.' Rory paused. 'Like a duck to water.'

Asha groaned. 'That was a terrible joke, Rory.'

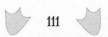

Rory's eyes twinkled. 'She's been here at the quack of dawn almost every morning.'

Asha slapped her hand against her forehead, as Katie and Mum giggled.

Rory winked. 'I've been saving that one specially.' He glanced at Katie. 'Will you be all right giving the ducklings their eleven o'clock feed?'

Katie nodded.

Rory turned to Mum. 'Sorry I can't stop and chat, Bea. The vet's just arrived. But I hope we'll see you again.'

'You will.' Mum smiled. 'It's lovely here.'

Asha jumped to her feet. 'Why's Jim here, Rory?'

'Nothing to worry about,' Rory told her. 'He just wants to have a look at one of the sheep. Can you come and help round him up? He's in the field and he's being a fiend to catch.'

'I keep telling you we need a sheepdog!' Asha pulled on her wellies. 'Are you coming, Katie?'

Katie shook her head. 'I want to show Mum round the rest of the farm.'

Rory opened the door. 'Why don't you start with Billy? He's looking a bit glum.'

'See you later,' Asha said, following Rory into the yard.

'Come on, Katie.' Mum knelt beside the nest-box. 'Tell me who's who again. They all look the same to me.'

Happy to show off her ducklings, Katie started lifting each one by one. 'This is Charlie,' she said. 'He's got brown wing tips and a thick stripe of brown feathers right down the middle of his back. And this is Waddles.' She swapped Charlie for another duckling. 'He's nearly all yellow.'

Mum admired every one of them, and when Katie put the last duckling back she gave her a hug. 'They're very lucky ducklings, having you to look after them.'

Katie heard a tremble in Mum's voice. She looked up and saw tears in Mum's eyes.

'I'm sorry I've kept you off school so much when I haven't felt well.' Mum swallowed and glanced down at her hands. 'The truth is, I've been very depressed because I don't have a job any more.'

'I know.' Katie threw her arms around Mum. 'I just wish I could cheer you up.'

Mum pulled her away gently. 'It's not your job to cheer me up.' She took a tissue from her sleeve and dabbed away her tears. 'I had a lovely chat with Kerry last night and I've decided to go to the doctor and get some help.' She looked at Katie and gave her a watery smile. 'I'm going to get better and get you back to school as soon as half term's over.'

'But what about the farm?' Katie glanced at her ducklings. 'Will I have to stop coming?'

Mum shook her head. 'Kerry thinks it's important you stay at the farm. You can come at the weekends and in the evenings. The ducklings need you and it's good that you have somewhere you feel happy.'

'I feel happy when I'm with you,' Katie blurted.

'Thank you, darling.' Mum stroked Katie's hair. 'But I know it's not easy for you when I'm so sad. I promise I will get better.'

Katie felt a lump rising in her throat. Her eyes were hot with tears. They spilled over and she flung herself into Mum's arms. 'I love you, Mum, no matter what, but it would be brilliant if you were happy again.'

'I know, love.' Mum hugged her hard. 'I will be, soon, I know it.'

# Chapter Ten

Katie skipped down the high street.

'Wait for me!'

She looked over her shoulder at Mum, laughing as she ran to catch up. 'Come on, slowcoach!' Katie carried on skipping. Sunshine glinted off the shop windows and Katie beamed at the passers-by as she headed for City Farm. She'd been working there at weekends for the past month, and on occasional evenings when there was time. Mum had seen the doctor, just like she'd promised, and was slowly starting to feel better. She'd managed to take Katie to school every day and they hadn't been late once. And she'd started applying for jobs again. She'd even been for two interviews and, although she hadn't found a job yet, she was more determined than ever.

'Hurry up, Mum!' Katie spotted the City Farm sign. 'The ducklings will be waiting for us!'

Mum puffed after her. 'They're hardly ducklings any more!' She caught up as Katie reached the gate.

Now that they were four weeks old, the ducklings still had their yellow baby feathers, but they were too big to fit in the palms of Katie's hands. Today she was going to take them to the duck pond for their first swim.

Katie paused at the gate. 'I hope the big ducks don't bully them.'

'Oh, I think they'll be able to stick up for themselves,' Mum reassured her. 'They're feisty little things.'

'Hurry up, Katie!' Asha called from one of the diamond-paned barn windows. 'The ducks want to see the pond.'

Jack squeezed his head out beside Asha. 'Wolverine keeps following Kerry into the kitchen. He's going to end up as roast duck if you don't get a move on!'

Katie raced across the yard and into the barn. The ducklings had grown too big to stay in their box so Katie had cut a hole in the side so they could go in and out. Now they were waddling around the barn, stretching their wings and quacking.

Mum caught up, panting.

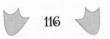

As soon as the ducklings saw Katie they came flapping over and crowded around her feet, quacking noisily.

Kerry appeared in the archway to the café. She was wearing an apron and wiping her hands on a tea towel. 'Thank goodness you're here!' She sounded really flustered. 'I can't keep them out of the café and Derrick Jarvis is due at eleven. If he finds ducklings swarming around in the kitchen, he'll close the café down for sure!'

'I'll take them to the pond,' Katie said.

'The sooner the better! I'm trying to bake and it's hard enough without ducks flapping at my feet. We need piles of cakes for when Mr Jarvis arrives. He's coming especially to see how we're coping now Daisy's gone.'

Jack shoved his hands in his pockets gloomily. 'I miss Daisy.'

'You miss her cakes!' Kerry sighed. 'Oh, *why* can't I bake? The more I try the worse I get.'

'Well, you'd better learn quickly,' Jack said. 'If you serve up burnt cakes today, Mr Jarvis will freak.'

Asha's eyes darkened with worry. 'Do you think he will close the café down?'

Kerry twisted her apron anxiously. 'If he thinks

the food's not fit to sell to the public, he'll certainly close the café down until we find someone to run it properly.'

'But we can't afford to close it,' Asha gasped.

'The café's the only bit of the farm that makes money,' Jack added.

Katie grabbed Mum's hand. 'Come on. Let's get the ducklings out of here so Kerry can cook.' She pulled open the door and headed outside. Quacking excitedly, the ducks followed.

Rory was parking the wheelbarrow next to the tool shed. 'You're here!' He strode across the yard. 'I've cleared the way to the pond. We just need you to lead them there.'

Asha and Jack tumbled out of the barn, more excited than the ducks.

'I bet Wolverine's the best swimmer,' Jack said.

Asha tugged his jacket. 'No way! Baby will be best!'

Katie headed along the path to the paddock, glancing backward to make sure the ducklings were following. She grinned as she saw the parade behind her. Six ducklings, Mum, Asha, Jack and Rory, all in a line, marching proudly behind.

She reached the paddock and followed the fence. Swift was galloping across the grass while Stanley grazed happily with Dusty the donkey. The old pony raised his head as they passed.

'Hello, Stanley,' Katie sang happily.

Stanley whinnied and whisked his tail and the ducks quacked noisily at him.

Ahead, the pond sparkled in the sunshine and, as they neared, the ducklings in the pen ran to the fence, squabbling and fighting. They were clearly trying to see who was quacking their way up the hill.

Katie turned and spoke to her ducklings. 'Say hello to your new friends.'

The ducklings quacked back at her.

Katie called to Rory. 'Shall I lead them straight into the pen?'

'You might as well,' Rory called over Asha's head. 'They've got to get used to each other eventually.'

Katie swung open the gate and shooed the older ducks away as her ducklings waddled in.

Buttercup, Waddles, Charlie, Scruffy, Baby and Wolverine huddled into a bunch and stared around, suddenly quiet.

The older ducks scurried back and forth, like anxious old women, staring at the newcomers. Then a mallard, his green feathered head gleaming in the sunshine, waddled forward and quacked at the ducklings. The ducklings quacked back and flapped their wings indignantly.

'It's OK, ducklings,' Katie soothed. 'They're just not used to you.'

She led them past the watching ducks to the water's edge while Asha, Jack, Mum and Rory let themselves into the pen and watched.

'Go on.' Katie waved the ducklings towards the pond, but they stayed on the bank, glancing first at her, then at the water.

Rory chuckled. 'I think you're going to have to show them what to do.'

Katie blinked at him. 'You want me to go into the water?'

Mum held up her hands. 'You know they'll follow you anywhere.'

Katie looked at her feet. She hadn't had time to change into her wellies. She couldn't wade into the water in her trainers.

'Have mine.' Rory crossed the pen and slid off his wellies.

Katie grinned up at him. 'Thanks, Rory.' She quickly undid her trainers and slid her feet into Rory's huge black boots. While Rory stood on the grass in his socks, she began to wade into the water.

The edge of the pond was slippery and she wobbled.

Asha dashed to her side and grabbed her hand. 'I've got you!'

Holding onto Asha, Katie edged deeper into the pond. As she found her footing, the water pressed harder against the sides of Rory's wellies.

The old ducks watched, murmuring to themselves as if they couldn't believe their eyes. The ducklings stared at her, shifting nervously along the bank.

'How are the ducklings doing!' A voice called from the paddock. Kerry was crossing the grass toward them.

'Katie's showing them how to get their feet wet,' Rory called back.

Kerry reached the fence and leaned over. 'They don't look very impressed.'

The ducklings quacked at Katie and sidled further along the shore. Katie let go of Asha's hand and beckoned to the ducklings. 'Come on, little ducklings, it's lovely out here!'

To her surprise, Wolverine jumped into the water. He landed with a splash and started paddling toward her.

'Come on, Wolverine!' Katie beckoned him closer, as the water lapped close to the top of Rory's wellies.

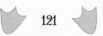

Jack cheered. 'Go, Wolverine!'

Asha waved at Baby. 'Go on, Baby!' she urged. 'Show him how *real* swimming's done.'

Baby flapped her wings and slithered down the bank, splashing into the water. Buttercup followed, Waddles right behind. Then Charlie and Scruffy launched themselves into the pond with a splash.

'Well done, Katie!' Mum called. 'You've raised six fine swimmers.'

Katie felt a rush of happiness as she stood in the pond, the ducklings bobbing around her. The water shimmered, reflecting glittering blue sky.

Asha crouched at the side of the pond and watched while Jack called out to Wolverine, 'Try diving, Wolverine!'

Wolverine floated past Jack, then ducked his head under the water, his tail bobbing up into the air.

'Nice one, Wolverine!'

Baby swam past Wolverine's tail, her beak in the air. Asha laughed. 'You're right, Baby. He's just showing off!'

One by one, the older ducks waddled up to the edge of the pond and slid in. Before long, the pond was busy with ducks. The ducklings circled Katie, then gradually began to move away, swimming among the older ducks and exploring the plants at the edge of the water.

Katie stuck out her elbows and started flapping. 'Quack, quack!'

Mum burst into laughter. 'Katie, you look so funny!'

Katie giggled as Mum took her camera out of her pocket and snapped a picture.

'I'm going to get this framed,' Mum declared.

'Get an extra copy for the barn wall,' Kerry called from the fence.

As Katie grinned proudly, she heard a distant beep. 'What's that?' She held up a hand and the others listened.

An alarm was screeching from the barn.

'It's the smoke alarm!' Kerry wailed. 'In the barn!' She looked at her watch. 'But the muffins shouldn't be ready for another ten minutes!'

Katie's heart lurched. She could see smoke wafting from one of the barn windows. Something was burning!

# Chapter Eleven

'Something's on fire!' Katie waded out of the pond and kicked off Rory's wellies.

Kerry leaped from the fence and raced down the field. Jack and Asha hurtled after her.

Mum dashed out of the pen. 'I'd better go and help.'

'Will the ducklings be all right if I leave them?' Katie pushed her feet into her trainers.

'I reckon so.' Rory glanced at the ducklings, swimming happily among the other ducks. 'You can fetch them later.'

Katie was already out of the gate and heading down the path to the barn.

Mum was rounding the corner ahead of her. Heart hammering, Katie caught her up at the barn. They

 124

raced inside.

'What's burning?' Katie called to Asha and Jack.

They didn't need to answer. Kerry came out of the kitchen in oven mitts, holding a tray of blackened, smoking muffins.

'They're toast,' Jack groaned.

'Oh, Kerry. You poor thing!' Asha stared at the muffins in dismay. 'What happened?'

'I set the oven at *two* hundred and seventy-five degrees instead of *one* hundred and seventy-five degrees.' Kerry's face crumpled. 'What's Mr Jarvis going to say?'

'He'll close the café for sure,' Jack sighed.

Kerry's eyes glistened, as though she was about to cry.

'Not necessarily.' Mum strode across the barn, rolling up her sleeves. 'Jack! Asha! Open every window you can find. We need to get rid of this burning smell. Katie, follow me!' She marched past Kerry.

Katie ran after her as she headed into the kitchen.

Kerry trailed in after them, holding her muffins. 'What are you doing?'

'How long till Mr Jarvis arrives?' Mum asked briskly.

'Half an hour,' Kerry answered blankly. 'Why?'

'That's plenty of time to make some more cakes!' Mum started opening cupboards and peering inside. 'Where's your flour. I'll need bowls, baking powder, cocoa, a whisk.'

Kerry slid her charcoal muffins onto the side and began grabbing ingredients from the pantry.

'Katie, turn the oven to one hundred and eighty degrees,' Mum said. 'We've got baking to do.'

Katie quickly flicked the oven knob, then hurried to a drawer and pulled out all the whisks and spatulas she could find.

Asha skidded into the kitchen. 'We've opened the windows,' she panted.

'Good.' Mum didn't turn round. She was already measuring margarine into a mixing bowl. 'You can be in charge of the brownies. Come and start mixing this.'

As Asha hurried to Mum's side, Katie threw her a wooden spoon. Asha caught it and started beating the margarine while Mum added sugar and said, 'Tell me when it's pale and creamy and I'll add the other ingredients.' She moved on to another mixing bowl and began measuring out more sugar. 'Katie, can you remember how to make fairy cakes.'

Katie nodded, picking up a spoon. Mum had taught her how to bake them as soon as she was old enough to stir.

Mum slid the bowl toward her. 'That's your job, then. Jack?'

Jack popped his head round the door.

'I need you to crumble up some biscuits.' Mum glanced at Kerry. 'Do you have any biscuits?'

Kerry nodded, then turned to Jack. 'Fetch the packet from the top drawer of my desk.'

Jack disappeared, returning a minute later with a packet of digestives.

'Great!' Mum was melting butter in a pan. 'Crumble them into smallish chunks.'

'Here.' Katie paused from whisking sugar and butter and passed Jack a bowl.

Kerry shuffled her feet. 'What can I do?'

'Tell me where the eggs are,' Mum said.

'Eggs?' Kerry's face froze. 'I used the last of them in the muffins.'

Mum took her pan off the heat and stared at Kerry. 'This is a farm, isn't it?'

Kerry nodded.

'And you have hens?'

Kerry gasped. 'Of course!' She undid her apron and draped it over Mum's shoulder. 'I'll be back in five minutes.'

'Make it two!' Mum called, as Kerry disappeared out of the back door.

Katie frowned, puzzled. 'Where's she going?'

Jack grinned. 'To fetch eggs, of course. The hens will have laid some during the night.'

'Of course!' Katie began to smile. She glanced at Mum, leaning over the stove. She hadn't seen her look so excited for ages.

'What do I do now?' Asha's bowl was full of richly creamed cake mix.

'Can you use the scales?' Mum asked her.

Asha nodded.

'Weigh out three lots of flour,' Mum said. 'A hundred grams for the first bowl…'

As Mum issued instructions, Katie focused on her fairy cakes. Her arm ached from stirring but she was glowing with happiness. Her ducklings were swimming and her mum was baking! She just hoped it would be enough to save the café from Mr Jarvis.

Thirty minutes later, Kerry looked at her watch. 'Mr Jarvis will be here any minute.'

Mum glanced at the oven. 'Don't worry, they'll be ready.' As she spoke the timer pinged and Mum reached for the oven door. 'Are the tables all wiped?'

Asha nodded. 'And I've put a little vase of flowers on every one.'

'It looks really pretty.' Katie had swept the café floor and opened up the visitors' door that led straight onto the yard to let the fresh spring sunshine in.

'I'll finish up in here,' Mum said. 'Why don't you go and greet Mr Jarvis.'

Kerry looked at her. 'I can't thank you enough, Bea.'

Mum waved her away. 'It was nothing. I'm just glad I could help.'

As Katie followed Kerry out into the café, Asha grabbed her hand. 'I hope Mr Jarvis likes everything.'

Katie squeezed Asha's fingers. 'So do I.'

A shadow darkened the café entrance.

A grey-haired man in a grey suit stood, frowning, on the doorstep. He was holding a clipboard and tapping his foot as he scanned the café. 'Empty counters,' he muttered. He stared at the bare cake shelves beside the till, then made a note on his clipboard. 'Very disappointing.'

'Mr Jarvis.' Kerry greeted him with an outstretched hand.

Mr Jarvis ignored it and brushed past her. 'You obviously haven't replaced Mrs Bainbridge yet. I'm

afraid we need to have a serious talk.'

Katie watched him stride through the café and into the barn. Kerry chased after him, her hair-beads jangling.

'He's such a grump,' Asha muttered.

Katie chewed nervously on her thumbnail. 'It sounds like he's already made up his mind about the café.'

Would Mum's cakes be enough to change it?

# Chapter Twelve

Katie and Asha tiptoed over to the archway and peered into the barn.

'The cakes are on their way.' Kerry hurried after Mr Jarvis. 'We're just a little behind.'

'Are you waiting for a delivery?' Mr Jarvis paused to make another note on his clipboard. 'I thought the café prided itself on its *home* baking.'

'It does!' Kerry cried. 'We've baked everything in the farm kitchen this morning.'

Jack crept up behind Katie and Asha. 'What's he doing?'

'Being mean to Kerry – as usual,' Asha growled.

Mr Jarvis sat down at Kerry's desk. Then he swept her papers aside and slammed his clipboard down. 'This isn't good enough,' he said loudly.

'Mr Jarvis!' Kerry stooped to pick up the papers he'd sent fluttering onto the floor. 'I realize the café has had its ups and downs since Daisy left.'

'As far as I can see it's all been *downs*,' Mr Jarvis snapped. 'It's just not sustainable.'

Jack whispered in Katie's ear. 'Your mum said the brownies are ready. She's about to put them on the counter. Everything looks delicious.'

'I hope Mr Jarvis will think so,' Katie whispered back. 'He sounds very cross.'

'Look at these figures.' Mr Jarvis waved a print-out under Kerry's nose. 'If the café keeps on sending in receipts like this, the farm will be bankrupt within the year.'

'But we won't,' Kerry pleaded. 'The café always struggles in the winter, but now summer's on the way there'll be more visitors.'

'But visitors want *food*,' Mr Jarvis spat. 'A few pens of mangy animals won't exactly pull the crowds in.'

'Our animals aren't mangy!' Katie exclaimed.

Mr Jarvis span round. 'What?' His eyes blazed at Katie.

Asha stepped forward. 'She said our animals aren't mangy!'

'No, they're not,' Jack added.

Mr Jarvis shook his head and sighed. 'Whoever said that you should never work with children or animals was a very wise man indeed!'

Katie heard plates clatter down on the counter behind her. She glanced over her shoulder and saw Mum putting out piles of brownies, cakes and muffins. The smell made her mouth water. She nudged Asha. 'Look!'

Asha turned and followed her gaze. 'Wow, they look great!'

'They smell even better!' Jack sniffed the air and grinned.

'Well?' Mr Jarvis was glowering at Kerry. 'Aren't you even going to offer me a cup of coffee?'

'O-of course,' Kerry stammered.

'The cakes are ready,' Katie said.

Kerry looked up, relief flooding her face as she caught sight of the plates of goodies over Katie's shoulder. Mum hurried behind the big coffee machine and started pulling levers and turning knobs.

'Come this way.' Kerry waved Mr Jarvis into the café.

Katie rushed to pull out a chair for him. 'There's a lovely view of the pens from here,' she told him as he sat down.

The coffee machine hissed and gurgled.

'I'll have a cappuccino,' Mr Jarvis muttered.

Katie rushed to the counter. Clouds of steam billowed round Mum. 'Can you work that thing?' she whispered.

Kerry leaned past her. 'Be careful, that coffee machine is a monster!'

Mum held a jug of milk under a shiny silver pipe until it began to froth. 'I paid my way through college working one of these old things.' She poured the milk into a cup of thick black coffee and handed it to Katie. 'Take him this,' she whispered. 'I'll bring some cakes over.'

Butterflies swarmed in Katie's stomach as she carried Mr Jarvis's coffee to his table.

He sniffed as she put it down next to him. 'Any chance of a cake – now they're *finally* ready.'

'I'll bring some over,' Mum called.

Kerry crossed the café to join Mr Jarvis while Mum piled brownies, muffins and fairy cakes onto a plate. 'I do hope you'll enjoy our *home* baking.' Kerry pulled out a chair and sat down.

'Here we are.' Mum marched breezily over to Mr Jarvis and held the plate under his nose.

Mr Jarvis grabbed a brownie. They all watched as

he took a bite.

Katie held her breath.

As he chewed, his face completely changed. It reminded Katie of watching a film of a flower unfurling. First of all his brow unfurrowed, then he blinked and widened his eyes, and finally his mouth curled up into a smile. 'But – but – this is *delicious*!' he exclaimed. 'How? I mean, where… ?' He took another bite. 'Did you really make these in the café kitchen?'

Kerry beamed. 'Yes,' she said proudly. 'And the eggs came from our own hens. They couldn't be fresher.'

Mr Jarvis narrowed his eyes. 'Hmm, I had no idea you were such a good cook, Kerry.'

'Oh, I wasn't the one in charge of the baking.' Kerry nodded at Mum. 'She was.'

Mr Jarvis looked at Mum properly for the first time. 'And who are you?'

Kerry interrupted before Mum could reply. 'She's our new café manager. She started today.'

Mum looked at her, startled. 'I am?'

Kerry stared at her pleadingly. *Say yes!* she mouthed.

'Oh, yes, sorry.' Mum grinned. 'I am.' She shook Mr Jarvis's hand. 'I'm Bea. Pleased to meet you.'

Katie felt little shivers of excitement. Had that

really just happened? Had Kerry really just offered Mum a job? And had Mum really said yes?

Asha raced over to Katie and squeezed her hand. 'That's brilliant!' she squeaked in her ear. 'Now City Farm will have the best cakes in the world!'

Mr Jarvis took another big bite of his brownie, causing his cheeks to bulge like a hamster. They all watched anxiously until he finally stopped chewing. 'Well, if this is anything to go by, maybe the café isn't in as much trouble as I thought.'

Kerry nodded and grinned. 'With Bea doing the baking we'll soon have people flocking to the farm.'

Mr Jarvis got to his feet and arranged his face back into a frown. 'I'll be wanting to see a big improvement on those receipts, mind.'

'Don't you worry, Mr Jarvis,' Mum said. 'I'll see that you do.'

Katie wanted to burst with happiness. Mum looked so happy and confident; exactly how she used to before she got so sad.

'Right, then.' Mr Jarvis picked up his clipboard. 'I'd better be off. Some of us have proper jobs to do, you know.'

Kerry looked at Mum and raised her eyebrows.

Then Mr Jarvis stopped and looked at Mum. 'Er,

I don't suppose I could take a selection of your cakes with me? For, er – work purposes.'

'Work purposes?' Mum said. Katie could tell she was trying really hard not to smile.

'Yes. I, er, will need to let my colleagues at the council know the results of my visit here today and I, er—'

'You wanted them to taste the cakes too,' Mum cut in.

'Yes. That's it. Yes,' Mr Jarvis spluttered.

'More like he wants more for himself,' Asha whispered in Katie's ear, causing her to giggle.

'No problem at all, Mr Jarvis,' Mum said, hurrying back to the counter. 'I'll put some in a bag for you. I mean, for *your colleagues*.'

'Right, yes, you do that.' Mr Jarvis followed Mum over to the counter, his face bright red.

'Look, he's actually embarrassed,' Asha whispered.

Mum handed him a bag of cakes. Mr Jarvis grabbed it and rushed to the door.

'Thank you,' he muttered, before racing out.

'He said thank you!' Kerry gasped, as soon as he was out of earshot. 'In all the years I've worked here, he's never once said thank you.'

'Your cakes must taste amazing!' Asha said to

137

Katie's mum. She looked at the remaining cakes longingly.

'They do,' Kerry said. 'And I think it's time we all tried them too – for work purposes, of course!'

As they all burst out laughing, Rory came striding into the café. 'What the heck's happened?' he said. 'I just saw old Jarvis leaving and he actually smiled at me and asked me how I was!'

'Bea's baking is what's happened,' Kerry said, offering him a brownie.

'It was so cool!' Asha exclaimed, helping herself to a chocolate muffin. 'He was being really mean as usual but then he tried one of Katie's mum's cakes and he went all weird and almost friendly!'

'Is that right?' Rory grinned at Katie's mum.

Mum nodded shyly and Katie felt so proud she wanted to jump up and down.

'And Bea has very kindly said that she'll be the new café manager,' Kerry said.

'Now that,' said Rory, sitting down, 'is very good news indeed.' He took a bite of his brownie and Katie watched as his twinkly eyes widened and he started to nod his head. 'Well, I'll be—'

'Aren't they delicious?' Asha said through a mouthful of muffin.

'Awesome!' Jack sighed as he chomped on a brownie.

Katie came and joined them at the table. 'Are the ducklings OK?' she asked Rory.

Rory nodded. 'Aye, they're sound. I've left them having a swim with the others. They're like one big happy family.'

As Mum came to sit next to her and Katie looked around the table at all of her new friends she realized that this is what City Farm felt like to her too – one big, happy family.

# Epilogue

'Hi, Mum.' Katie wandered into the café and sank down at one of the tables. She was exhausted after helping muck out the stables.

Mum looked up from behind the counter where she was slicing a three-layer chocolate cream cake into thick wedges. Her eyebrows shot up. 'You can't bring animals in here!' she gasped. 'What would Mr Jarvis say?'

'Animals?' Katie stared back at Mum, puzzled. She'd left Stanley and Swift munching hay in their stalls.

Mum pointed at her feet.

Katie looked down and burst out laughing. 'Sorry, Mum! I forgot!' The ducklings were all flapping around her feet. Even though they were now two months old, they still followed her everywhere. She'd been so eager to come and see Mum she hadn't noticed them follow her into the café.

Baby pecked at some crumbs on the floor. Charlie and Waddles chased each other around the legs of her chair. Buttercup and Scruffy looked up at her and quacked.

'You're meant to wait outside,' Katie scolded.

Wolverine shook out his feathers huffily. He'd grown into a really handsome duck over the past weeks, but even though he'd lost his brown and yellow duckling feathers Katie could still recognize him.

'Go and sit outside on a bench.' Grinning, Mum shooed her toward a door. 'I'll bring you a milkshake and a piece of cake.'

'Can Asha and Jack have one too? They've almost finished mucking out Cynthia.'

'Of course,' Mum smiled.

'And, Mum?'

Mum reached into a cupboard and pulled out a loaf of bread. 'I know! Don't forget to bring some bread for the ducks!'

# CHARACTER PROFILE

ANIMAL: Ducklings
ANIMAL NAMES: Wolverine,
Baby, Buttercup, Waddles,
Charlie and Scruffy.

## NOTES:

All six ducklings are doing well and they're easy
to tell apart now.

- Wolverine likes swimming and is always splashing
  about in the pond.
- Baby is the biggest and she's always coming into
  the cafe, looking for food.
- Charlie is the naughtiest, he likes chasing his
  brothers and sisters around.
- Waddles is the fastest and Charlie can never
  catch him!
- Buttercup is the prettiest duckling and she's
  growing her adult feathers already.
- Scruffy is the noisiest and he's always
  quacking loudly.

Read on for a sneak peek of the next City
Farm adventure...

# Laura and Silky

Laura could feel the warm glow of the morning sun on her cheeks and arms. She screwed her eyes shut and pictured the light dancing over the photos that were pinned to her bedroom wall – photos of her friends pulling silly faces, photos of her mum and dad on holiday, photos of Laura herself, laughing into the camera.

*When I open my eyes, I'll be able to see them*, thought Laura. *This time, I know I will.* She took a deep breath, then counted: *one, two, three!* And her eyelids flew open.

Nothing. Still nothing. Only darkness.

*Next time*, thought Laura. Next time. She'd tested herself a million times over the last few months, ever since she'd woken up in hospital with meningitis and discovered she was blind. Each time she hoped it would be different – that she'd open her eyes and see all the wonderful shapes and colours around her, just as she had before. But it hadn't happened.

She could hear footsteps now, soft light footsteps coming up the stairs. *Mum*, thought Laura. *She's carrying something.* She heard the faintest clink as her mother approached the bedroom. *A tray. She must be bringing me breakfast.*

There was a waft of cooler air as the door opened. 'Morning, sweetheart!' her mum greeted her. 'I've brought you a treat today, your favourite – toasted waffles with maple syrup. And some freshly squeezed orange juice.'

'Ooooh, lovely! Thanks, Mum.'

The rich, sweet smell filled the room. Laura pulled back the bed covers, swung her legs out of bed and stepped over to her little table. She knew exactly how many strides she should take and how far back she should pull her chair.

'I'm putting the tray on the table,' her mother told her.

Laura imagined her bending down with the tray, remembering her mum's dark-brown hair, cut into a neat bob that swung around her cheeks, her warm smile and her sparkling grey-blue eyes.

'Now,' said Mum. 'The waffles are at the front of the tray. And your orange juice is just to the side.'

'It's OK, Mum, I can work it out,' said Laura, reaching eagerly for the juice.

'No – Laura, careful!' cried her mum.

Too late. There was a crash, and Laura heard the drip-drip-drip of the juice pouring onto the carpet. The glass had been closer than she'd thought, and she'd knocked her hand right into it.

'Sorry,' said Laura, frustrated. 'I'm really sorry—'

'Never mind,' her mum replied soothingly. 'Don't worry. It's not much. I'll soon clean it up.'

Laura felt helpless. 'I wish my eyes would hurry up and get better again,' she said.

Her mum was silent for a moment. Then Laura heard her lean forward and felt her hand wrapping around her fingers. 'Laura,' she said quietly. 'You know what the doctors said, sweetheart.'

'I know what they *said*,' said Laura. 'But I don't have to believe them, do I?'

Another silence. At last her mum replied, 'Well … I know it's really, really hard, but it might be better if you did, you know.'

The juice was still dripping, but more slowly now. Drip … drip … drip. Laura listened to it. She thought of how everything she could hear and smell was slowly seeming louder, and more intense.

And then, suddenly, it hit her. *This is my world now. I'm never going to see anything, ever again. This is it.*

She hadn't wanted to believe it. She knew the meningitis had made her seriously ill, but she'd survived. She'd got better. Against the odds, her whole body had got better – apart from her eyes; so why shouldn't they get better too?

Now, for the first time, she faced up to the truth. There was no point in testing herself every day, hoping her sight would come back again. There was no point in waiting for the big moment when her world would fill with light and colour.

'Laura? Are you all right?' Laura's mum sounded worried.

Two fat tears welled up in Laura's eyes. She felt them escape from each eye in turn, and roll down her cheeks. *Stupid eyes!* She thought. *They can still cry, but they can't see!* They'd never see. That wasn't going to change. Ever. Not for the rest of her life…

Read

# Laura and Silky

to find out what happens next!

HANDBOOK

## CITY FARM RULES:

*Lots of people visit City Farm everyday. Follow these simple rules to make sure that everyone enjoys themselves.*

🖐 Treat people – and animals – with respect and kindness.

🖐 Help out and join in! If you can see someone needs a hand, offer to help them.

🖐 Don't feed the animals, some of them are on special diets, and different food will upset their tummies.

🖐 Wash your hands! Most of the City Farm animals like to be held and stroked, but you should always wash your hands afterwards.

🖐 Have fun!

# OUR GUINEA PIGS:

*Bubble and Squeak are our guinea pigs. They're very friendly and love being held and petted every day.*

🐾 Guinea pigs originally come from South America and usually live until they are five or six years old.

🐾 Guinea pigs are very social creatures and Bubble and Squeak would get very lonely if they didn't have each other. They like having lots of hay and straw to burrow in, and toilet-roll tubes to use as tunnels.

🐾 Guinea pigs are active up to 20 hours per day and sleep only for short periods.

🐾 Guinea pigs make lots of different noises which mean different things. When they're excited they make lots of squeaking 'wheek' sounds and they purr when they're being stroked.

## Our Equines:

*City Farm is lucky enough to have a pony called Stanley,
an ex-racehorse called Swift and a donkey called Dusty. Horses
and donkeys take a lot of looking after.*

Our horses and donkeys need to be mucked out every morning, and given a pile of fresh straw for their beds.

They have small feeds at breakfast and lunchtime, and each have a net full of hay in the evening. During the day they are 'turned out' into the field for at least six hours so that they can graze on the grass.

We always check that there are no holes in the fencing, and no broken glass or poisonous plants before they are turned out into the paddock.

In the winter, Dusty, Stanley and Swift have stable rugs on their backs so they don't get cold.

# OUR PIG:

*Cynthia is City Farm's Tamworth pig. She loves playing football!*

🐾 Pigs are actually very clean. When Cynthia rolls in the mud it's because she's hot. Pigs can't sweat, so they cover themselves in cool mud, which cools them down and protects their skin from the sun.

🐾 Pigs are also very smart, and they learn tricks faster than dogs. They like to have toys like a football to keep them entertained.

🐾 Tamworth pigs are a gingery-orange colour, and they originally come from the UK.

🐾 Pigs have such a good sense of smell that they can find things buried underground.

🐾 It is actually illegal to give pigs scraps from the kitchen.

# OUR GOATS:

*City Farm has five goats – dairy goats Nelly and Nancy, male goats Billy and Bramble, and a new goat, naughty little Basher.*

- Dairy goats need milking every day. More people in the world drink goats' milk than cows' milk. Goat's milk makes delicious cheeses.

- Goats can live between 12 and 16 years.

- Goats only have teeth on their bottom jaw, the top is a hard palate.

- Goats are often very good at escaping their pens – like Basher – so we have to make sure their enclosures are secure.

- Baby goats are called kids, and goats can have up to six kids per litter.

## Our Chickens and Ducks:

*There are lots of chickens and ducks at City Farm, and more ducklings and chicks hatch every year.*

🌷 Chickens and ducks need a shed to sleep in at night, otherwise they might get eaten by foxes.

🌷 Very few ducks actually "quack", but ducks do make a wide range of noises.

🌷 Ducks have webbed feet that act like paddles, and their feathers are waterproof.

🌷 Chickens preen their feathers every day, and like to take dust baths in the farmyard.

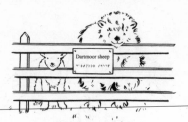

# OUR SHEEP:

*Curly and Lizzie are City Farm's Greyface Dartmoor Sheep. They have floppy fringes that fall over their eyes and are very woolly and cuddly!*

Female sheep are called ewes, male sheep are called rams, and baby sheep are called lambs.

Sheep like to live together in a flock. If one moves, the others will follow. When people copy what each other do without thinking, it's called being a sheep.

Sheep have to be shorn every year, and their wool is spun into thread that makes clothes, blankets, and lots of other things.

Sheep were some of the first animals to be domesticated by people.